# FILOMENA

## A SCAF

GW00374588

## BY LA

Editing by Eleanor Lloyd-Jones of Shower of Schmidt

Cover by Book Cover Kingdom

laurarossiauthor@gmail.com

This is a work of fiction. Names, characters, businesses, places, events and incidents are either the of the author's imagination or used in a fictitious manner. Any resemblance to actual persons, living or dead, or actual events is purely coincidental.

Warning: this book contains dark mafia themes.

2

I dedicate this book to my brother Carlo and his lovely girlfriend Olga.

And to sacrifice, dark times and tables finally turning.

# PROLOGUE

Lie to me. Tell me it's not too late to change; tell me to fight back; tell me everything will be okay in the end. Lies I can take: they help me push through. Lies are what got me to this point. I survived the truth holding on to what wasn't real.

Lie to me, and I'll pretend I believe you.

Pretend.

Yes, that's what I do—that's what life taught me. Pretend you are okay, pretend you are in control, pretend nothing hurts you… until one day, you are put face to face with your lies—the reality of your existence—and you can't cover it up; you can't hide or find your way out. Because in the end, the truth will always find its way back to you, destroying the life you've worked so hard to build for yourself and your loved ones.

The truth—that's what I'd seen in Andrea's cold, guarded eyes.

I'd seen the consequences of my mistakes. I'd seen a woman hurting, fighting for her son. I'd looked into her eyes and had seen myself. God knows I'd pretended it wasn't true, but the truth had slapped me cold. She'd told me what deep down I already knew, and the words she wasn't brave enough speak, I'd heard anyway: in her long silences, her soft sobs and pleas.

I'd seen a young mother, desperate to protect her son.

I'd looked into her eyes and had seen the old me.

Life has this strange habit of repeating itself. Not only the ghosts of my past and the mistakes of my youth haunt me day and night, but I've had to witness my children living through the same fate as mine—the children of my children…

I can stop this. I can.

*"I need you to help me; I need you to help me save Eddy." Andrea looks at me hopefully. I am the only person she is allowed to speak with. Alejandro keeps her isolated, far away from the outside world. She has no other choice. I am the only person she can trust, her last chance to save her son, but I am also Alejandro's mother.*

*"You can't ask me to betray my son." I shake my head as tears pool in her light blue eyes.*

*Pain. I see it bloom inside her. It's like looking into a mirror—just like me years back. And all of a sudden it all comes back to me, what I've done, what I've had to do to try to save my son.*

*I close my eyes tight and push away those memories, my breathing changing as thoughts of Alejandro and my husband try to knock down the wall I'd been so careful to build over the years.*

*No. No thinking about the past. I did what I had to, to protect Alejandro. I had to try, even though it didn't work. I had been too late.*

*But it's not too late for her, for them. Eddy is still a child—she can save him.*

*My eyes lock with Andrea's then.*

*"Please, please help me. I can't watch Eddy live like this. Hatred will consume him. He'll grow up seeking revenge, wanting to destroy everything and everyone around him. He'll grow up to be like Alejandro…" her voice trails off, but I know we are both thinking the same thing.*

Like a monster.

*I know what my son is. I know what he's become: bloody and merciless like his father.*

*I can't save him. I am too late.*

*After years, I find myself at the same crossroad, standing right in the middle of it with no other choice but make a choice and with no guarantee I'll make the right decision. But I can't pretend everything will be okay. Not this time. I have to do something. I have to try.*

*Do it for the family. Do it for your conscience. Don't turn your head the other way until it's too late, not this time. Make all the wrong right.*

*It doesn't take me long to decide. I know what needs to be done: my guts have been telling me for so long, no matter how good I am at pretending, at lying to myself and the world. Deep down I have known this day would come—the day I have to stop Alejandro myself.*

So I helped her. I helped Andrea. I'd gone against my own son for something greater: to protect my grandson from the insanity of his father.

Alejandro had been completely out of control: dangerous for himself and others. He wouldn't listen to anyone, he couldn't see things clearly. Revenge and hatred had been controlling his mind.

He'd been about to destroy an innocent child.

That day, I made a decision that changed the course of the events. I'd helped Andrea—played her game until it all blew up in our faces and the lies came to an end. I'd nearly lost them both: my son and my grandson. I nearly had. My heart had stopped when that gunshot was fired.

Days like this one, where I sit alone in a waiting room, I wish it had. I wish my heart had stopped together with Alejandro's. I wish that bullet had have hit me, too.

"Signora Filomena De la Crux." A young, distinguished police officer enters the room. I eye him quietly, as he walks to the table and takes a seat across from me, folder in hand.

He stares at me, like he knows me all too well—no need to open those files. He knows who I am, what I am and thinks he knows what I've just seen.

My son's death.

*You have no idea—no idea what I've seen or been through.*

I want to tell him exactly that, but I don't. I sit there, patiently, knowing there's always time to speak and tell the truth. Now it's not the time.

"Would you like to tell me what happened? What happened in that abandoned factory, your side of the story?" he asks, and I smile a little, meeting his stare.

"My side of the story…" I waver as the last fifty years of my life flash before my eyes.

# CHAPTER 1

Don't feel bad for me. I'm a sinner. I wear the cross. Not because I'm worthy of it but because I need it more than anyone else, more than any faithful, pure heart.

I need it like any other sinner, as a shield to help me not fall into the vortex of sin.

When I married Alonso De la Crux, I'd known what I'd been walking into—I'd known who he was.

'The Bloody Columbian' they'd called him. He'd been feared and respected by everyone in Rome, including my father, who had been the one to introduced us. My father, The Duke Antonio Del Monte, had been one of the last aristocrats in Italy: a very powerful and influential politician. Whatever had happened in Rome had been none other than my father's will. Nobody had been able to move a single stone without his approval.

An aristocratic, political Mafioso—my father.

*"I give you this, you give me that."*

*"I let you build here, you give me permission to operate and take my trade there."*

The glamorous parties had been nothing but a cover up. My father had used them to make business with other powerful men like him. Alonso De la Crux had come along to one of those soirees.

*"There's someone I'd like you to meet," he says to me, gently guiding me through the garden, greeting the guests sipping their cocktails by the pool.*

*"This is Alonso De la Crux, the son of one of my most trustworthy business partners," he tells me.*

A thirty-something-year-old man, dressed in a dark grey suit, his hair styled back with gel—like it was so popular in those days—with a flashy white smile and dark penetrating eyes. I'd known who he was: magnetic and charismatic, a smooth talker.

*"Signorina Del Monte," Alonso takes my hand and bends forward, his lips stopping inches from it like a real gentleman. His eyes swallow mine.*

*"I was told you were the prettiest girl in town, but I'd never have imagined you looked so beautiful." He straightens up, letting my hand slip away from his slowly—so slowly I feel his fingers run through mine.*

*"Grazie." I smile and tilt my head to the side, curious.*

I hadn't been the innocent young lady I looked. I'd known more than I cared to show, but in those days, girls were taught to pretend—not be bold and flirt with a good party. Still, I hadn't been able to bite my tongue.

*"I've heard stories about you." It comes out of my mouth before I can even think to play innocent.*

*"Good ones I hope." He nods, a crooked grin making his whole face twitch in a sensual smirk.*

Many, many women scattered around the world, also known as The Lord of Cocaine, a strong man, a ruler…

*"Interesting ones." I smile back, and Alonso beams at my boldness.*

*"And they are all true." He holds my stare and succeeds where every other man has failed up to now.*

9

*I look down, embarrassed, flushed.*


I'd felt a pull towards him instantly. I hadn't been sure why, but his voice had made me jump a little, my pulse speed up a little faster. I'd found it so difficult to say something then.

It had been the sixties, Italy, and I was a twenty-year-old girl who'd done nothing but go to school and church. I hadn't been allowed much else besides attending the exclusive tennis club on Sunday afternoons. I'd seen the same people every day, mingled with aristocrats and people from my same background—people my father had wanted me to see: sons and daughters of his friends.

Alonso had been everything I'd been looking for: older, foreign, interesting and deliciously dangerous, adventurous and proud… the way he'd held his head high—a little higher than the rest… Not because he'd had blue blood running in his veins, but because he'd been a self-made man.


*"My family is originally from Columbia. They moved to Italy a few years ago," he tells me when I ask about his upbringing.*

*"I've always wanted to visit South America," I comment, looking down, then up, into his eyes again, a soft smile playing on my lips.*

*"Perhaps one day," he murmurs cheekily, "you could be my guest."*

*A guest, in Alonso De la Crux's house. In Colombia. My heart flutters.*

*What a dream that would be.*


I'd wanted nothing more than to escape from Rome, run free and find a man that could give me the world. I'd continued to study him, mesmerized by this magnetic man who'd wanted to meet me so badly. Me: Filomena Del Monte, thin and fragile and fresh out of school.

It had been my very first encounter with the outside world, and I'd been drunk on his words.

I'd wanted to know about his country, his adventures. We'd stood there, at a corner of the pool, talking for so long that I hadn't even noticed until the end that my father had been looking at us from his table.

That was when the music changed and people had moved towards the small marquee they'd assembled on our lawn. Alonso had taken my hand—my heart in my mouth—and guided me towards the dancefloor.

Ah the sixties.

We'd danced cheek to cheek, one of his hands holding mine, the other one down my back. His finger touched my skin where my light blue dress had been slightly open on my spine, and I'd looked sideways at him. He'd smiled, holding that head high again.

I hadn't known I was his winnings; I hadn't known he'd come to collect.

The last man I really trusted had been my father.

He broke me the day he let that man dance me down to hell with him.

# CHAPTER 2

It sounds like I had been tricked into loving Alonso, and in a way I had. My father and Alonso's father had been good business partners: the Duke Del Monte had closed his eyes and smoothed the way for the De la Crux's drug trade in Rome, letting them settle nicely in the outskirts of the city. The De la Crux had paid him quite handsomely.

But alliances are always sort of fragile if based solely on money.

Money makes men cheaters, liars, untrustworthy… What could have been better than a marriage of convenience to strengthen the alliance between two families?

Alonso had easily complied. He'd set his eyes on me: the youngest daughter of Del Monte.

I know my father had tried to change his mind. I'd found out years later.

My sisters had all been the right age for marriage, but Alonso hadn't wanted to hear of it. He'd wanted me: the youngest, daddy's girl… I think he'd known how big of a sacrifice it would have been for my father to give up his youngest.

It had been a trade. I'd been part of the bargain—nothing but a product, an investment, a bridge between the two families.

I'd find out later I'd been sacrificed to seal a deal, not just to strengthen their trade. My father had given the De la Crux permission to get their hands on the building of new apartment blocks in a neighbourhood in Rome known as The Market. De la Crux had been able to launder their money in there and make more money out of it, but for how long? How long Del Monte would allow them to thrive, nobody had known.

Balances are so hard to achieve, but when blood and family are involved, the bonds are tighter.

*"We'll give you a part of the earnings; you'll be the richest man in the town. We can do so much together if our two strong families unite."*

Alonso had convinced him with time.

Money, money, money…

I'm yet to meet a man who won't get down on his hands and knees for money.

I hadn't been forced to love him. It had been easy to fall for Alonso. I'd had little experience with men: I'd only kissed one before—a school friend during gym class. We'd hidden behind the lockers.

Kissing Alonso had been completely different. He'd kissed me out in the open, no hesitation, no embarrassment, without hiding. He'd kissed me at a screening of Breakfast at Tiffany's under the stars.

Long and slow, he'd held my hand and whispered in my ears how beautiful I was.

I don't remember a single thing about that movie, about that night, other than his scent, his eyes, his tongue…

*"I can't concentrate much; I'm too distracted by you," he whispers in my ear, careful so no one could hear us.*

*My cheeks are on fire.*

*"Filomena, Filomena." His Spanish accent makes my name sound so alluring, exotic, foreign and sensuous, and when Alonso holds my hand as we walk back to his car later, shivers run down my back. The tips of his fingers trace down my wrist, and I turn my palm up and let him tickle my skin. I explore his hand too.*

*"Tell me, bella Filomena, have you ever kissed a man?" His dark eyes look straight into mine, one finger brushed against my pink lips.*

13

*I shake my head gently as he leans a little forward, stopping inches from my mouth, tilting his head a little as if studying me well.*

No, I had never kissed a man. A boy yes, but not a man like Alonso.

I'd lied, pretended I was the innocent young girl he wanted me to be—pretended I'd never been touched before—but I'd been so eager to explore, to venture out in the world and leave the restrictions of my house. I'd wanted to see everything and I'd wanted a man, determined and strong like Alonso, by my side.

*"You make me feel like I'm on top of the world," Alonso whispers. "Like I'm the luckiest man on Earth to have had the pleasure of taking out the most gorgeous woman I've ever set eyes on. Can I see you again?"*

*"Well, it depends," I murmur, my voice so fragile. I'm completely mesmerized by him, but I hide it well like a real woman should.*

*His lips touch mine for a moment and we both close our eyes. I hear him suck in a breath as his body moves a little closer.*

*Alonso stops and I look back up to him as he whispers, "Depends on what, mia bella Filomena?"*

*"On your intentions." I bite my lip a little, biting his too for how close we are.*

Tobacco and mint.

*I taste the world on his lips.*

*I want to smoke, too. I want to be free like him—like a man.*

*"What do you have to offer?" I tease, leaving that kiss hanging mid air between us.*

That's right, I'd wanted to know what was going to be in it for me.

14

Something had sparked in his eyes then, like I'd surprised him. Pleasantly surprised him. Maybe Alonso had been expecting a remissive, an innocent little girl, but I'd shown him my true colours.

I'd wanted to know where our dates were going to lead me, where he was going to take me.

I am the youngest daughter of Antonio De Monte, but I hadn't been shy or naïve back then.

The times had forced me to be quiet, to be a lady—never over the top, reserved and elegant. Never talk back to my father.

That night—that first date with Alonso De la Crux—had been my first night out on my own with my father's blessing, but don't think I hadn't sneaked out of the house before. I had, several times, listened in on my father's conversations with his 'business associates', while they'd lounged out in our garden.

I'd known what he was, what he did, and I'd known how important he was—how important we were in society.

I am the youngest but I'd had a very clear idea of the world outside those walls, outside of that neighbourhood.

To me, the world is divided into two categories: those who led and those who follow. We'd been the leaders, the strong ones, and I'd been proud of who I was.

I was a fool.


*"I'll make you my queen; I'll give you everything your heart desires, mia bella Filomena. We can rule the world together, what do you say?"*


I'd smiled and nodded. Exactly what I'd wanted, exactly what I'd been looking for: be a queen, be married to someone who could support me and give me a life better than the one I'd already been living.

Respect and power… I'd had my father's ambitious blood in me.

Alonso had sealed the deal with a kiss—my first kiss out in the open with a real man of honour.

He'd been the right man for me; he'd give me everything and made sure I could walk around and be respected by everyone. At all costs.

What did I tell you? No need to be sorry for me. I'm not innocent. I never was.

# CHAPTER 3

*"Volare, oh oh, cantare, oh oh oh. Nel blu dipinto di blu."*

Alonso hadn't left anything out.

He'd serenaded me under my window the night before our wedding in keeping with tradition, and Alonso had followed the rules of courtship to the letter. And to my father's approval.

I had been over the moon, happy he was keeping his promises, giving me everything I'd wanted.

The most prestigious wedding gown designed by top fashion designers, the trendiest location for our reception, flowers and diamonds in my hair… Eight hundred guests had been invited between family members, business associates and all the richest, most popular elite of Rome and surrounding areas.

I'd worn a long veil on the day, keeping my eyes low and calm as expected by a respectful virgin, but behind that thick veil I'd hidden my thirst for life. I'd finally been free, moving forward, getting out of my father's radar and out into the world.

I'd glided down the long central nave of the cathedral, never looking sideways, staring at one man and one man only: Alonso.

My father had gripped my arm a little tighter, but I'd ignored him.

I wasn't his, not anymore. He was handing me over to Alonso, he was striking a lifetime deal with the De la Crux and I was going to be queen. I'd been ready to rule on my terms—ready to have control over a man that was totally infatuated by me.

*"Be happy," he whispers, kissing me on the cheeks as the chorus sings Hail Mary. We are only a few steps from Alonso when I think my father, the impetuous, iron man that he is, has a moment—a moment of hesitation. His hand holds mine a little longer while I step up the altar, to my king.*

*Alonso's eyes dig right through the veil while the priest talks about love and commitment.*

*"I'm committed to making you the happiest, most satisfied woman in this world," he whispers leaning a little to the side as the chorus broke into another canto.*

*"I'm committed to making you the happiest, most satisfied man in this world," I whisper back, a hint of mischief in my voice.*

*"Once this is all over, I don't want to leave the bedroom for a week," he whispers again, just before the music stops playing and it is all quiet for a moment.*


The only sound in my ear had been my heart. It had pounded, my stomach twirling with excitement. I'd wanted to live so badly. I'd wanted to get out of that dress and make him mine, keep him between my legs for as long as he wanted to be there.

*The power of a woman lies between her legs.*

I'd read it in one of the books my father had forbidden me and my sisters to read, and for that particular reason I had gone out and bought it, 'The Sexual Education of a Modern Woman', and hidden it under two wooden tiles in the shed.

My sisters had obeyed; I'd disobeyed with a smile on my lips and had read the whole thing, three times, the last time being a few days before the wedding.

*Seduce him and he will let you do whatever you want.*

I had been used by all the men I knew: by my father for his business agreements; by Alonso for the same reason and for love and companionship. But I wasn't going to allow anyone to use me without getting something back—without using them too.


I do.

The words had been set in stone. We were a couple. More importantly, we were a family—two families that had come together—and we'd all got what we wanted.

My father's affairs had thrived; Alonso had had his back covered and his hands in the construction of The Market, while his men had sold his drugs around town undisturbed.

I'd been kept in the dark—or so they thought—but I'd known everything. Despite leading a quiet, respectful life, I'd known what they were up to and the balance had been perfect.

It had made everyone happy.

Alonso had kept his promises. I was his queen.

I'd had everything I'd wanted: a stylish lifestyle, luxuries, holidays in five-star resorts…

When in Rome, I'd spent my days with my lady friends, shopping in top boutiques in Via Del Corso or having coffee in Piazza Navona, flashing the gorgeous pieces of jewellery my husband had bought for me.

I was a lady—the wife of one of the most powerful gangsters in town and a descendant of a duke.

The institutions couldn't touch me even if they wanted to: people had respected me like I was a goddess.

I'd been young and superficial; I'd thought that was all that had mattered: to be respected and envied.

For the first year or so everything had been perfect, and I'd never questioned anything: what my husband did late at night, where he went or what sins marked his hands. He did what he'd had to do, I'd told myself.

And he'd kept me busy, very busy, in the bedroom. No matter what time he'd come back at night.


*"Mia bella Filomena," he whispers in my ears in the darkness of the room. "Wake up, mia bella Filomena. Your man is back, back between your legs."*

He would go for my neck and I'd giggle, opening my eyes, a little drowsy.

I was never able to resist him; he'd been such a fine man, my husband. Tall and strong, charismatic and so good with his mouth…

I couldn't get enough of him. We couldn't get enough of each other. I think lust and power had got to our heads. We'd done so well, getting richer by the minute. I was his favourite ally, he'd tell me. While he would strike deals at night, I would strike deals in a more refined, composed manner, bonding with the women of other gangsters.

*"I married the perfect woman," he tells me, unbuttoning my nighty, slipping one hand over my breast.*

# CHAPTER 4

Money is like a drug. You say you have enough, you tell yourself you can stop anytime, but it's a lie. If you are used to power and riches, you can't stop. You'll want to do anything to keep that status and expand your earnings.

Alonso had been a loose cannon. He'd become so strong, stretching his possessions across the city like a spiderweb. My father had told him more than once to stop pushing boundaries.

*"You are making our associates nervous. You need to stop."*

First warning.

Alonso had kept quiet and had taken it with a soft smile on his lips.

He hadn't been listening—too many possibilities to become richer, to take advantage and exploit the increasing drug trade. Not just cocaine and heroin, but LSD and cannabis.

Alonso had spread his trade with care and mastery. Until he upset other powerful gangsters and my father had to make peace.

He'd made a point of talking to Alonso once and for all; he'd planned to put an end to his little games of power.

*"Stop invading their territory. Stop sticking your nose in their business, stealing their space."*

Second warning.

Nobody had been smiling that time. I remember standing in one corner, eyeing both the men of my life as they'd silently stared at one another, neither of them ready to stand down.

*"Or?" Alonso glares.*

*"We'll start losing our connections, all the power we've earned so far," my father explains.*

*"Or we win and take everything—everything, Antonio. Broaden your horizons. We could control everything," Alonso says, his eyes gleaming with every word that comes out of his mouth.*

Control everything. Win.

*"Breaking the agreements, trying to kick our 'friends' out of the trade, will only give us trouble. It will set off a series of events—a war. We don't want that, Alonso. We don't. Trust me. We are thriving; business is good. We control Rome, but we need to throw bones to others, too. An unsatisfied person is a dangerous person—a potential enemy. We don't want enemies."*

My father had spent a long time talking to my husband.

He'd been more experienced.

He'd known what he was doing.

No need to upset anyone.

*"Sometimes we need to appreciate what we have and be satisfied with it."*

*"And sometimes we need to seize a chance, expand our interests, grow," Alonso cuts in.*

*"Not when it means going against our friends. People have trusted and respected me for years."*

*"Trust," Alonso laughs. "They respect you until you are of no use to them, until they find something better. We could do so much more on our own instead of sharing our interests with others."*

*"This is how I've built my business; this is how it has always been," my father snaps, his finger pressing against his chest, stressing the word 'I'.*

*A king marking his territory, his business, his rules.*

Stand down, Alonso.

22

*I watch them both, my eyes darting from one to the other .*

Stop.

*My breathing picks up.*

*Alonso seems to have listened. He lowers his eyes and I let out a deep breath. He is stepping down; he is going to apologize and my father will forgive him. Things will go back to normal.*

*But Alonso looks up again—confident, authoritarian—and I see in his stare what I should have seen back then, when I first met him: a born leader, just like my father. But a kingdom can only have one king—one man setting the rules.*

"Not good enough for me. I want more," *Alonso's voice shakes the room.*

*I look at my father instantly.*

*He stops pacing the room, his eyes wide.*

"Christ, Alonso. You need to stop pushing, you need to stop acting like you are on your own. We are in this together You can't walk around and do as you please. Things work when there's a balance; you are destroying that balance I've been building for years and for what? For a couple of hundred thousands more a week? We have millions, we have connections everywhere, in every sector, every corner of this damn city. Stop what you are doing or I swear to God I will stop you." *A threat, there it was.*

*A war.*

*I shake at the thought, my head moving sideways.*

No, no.

*A war and I am in the middle.*

"I'll wait for you outside, Filomena,"


Alonso hadn't bothered to say anything else to my father, not with words anyway, but that look in my husband's eyes had held a promise.

The conversation hadn't been over; it was just the beginning.

The beginning of a battle.

One more glare and he'd left the room. I'd stayed for a moment, my attention on my father.

Antonio Del Monte, severe and proud. He hadn't softened his broad, stiff shoulders when I'd run to him, both hands on his chest, mumbling a plea.

*"Don't fight Alonso, please don't..."*

*"I've given him everything he wanted. I can't let him destroy what I've built over the years, Filomena."*

He'd been right. My father had only been protecting his interests, but maybe Alonso being younger, he'd seen opportunities where my father hadn't. Maybe it could have been for the best; maybe some good could have come from his ideas.

*"Tell your husband to stop this nonsense, Filomena. And tell him to stop now or you'll end up a young widow. Not because I will hurt him but because our 'friends' will. He doesn't know what he's dealing with,"* my father tells me holding my hands, reading the worry in my eyes.

Alonso killed, Alonso punished for his delusions of grandeur.

Me alone, dressed in black, losing my husband for not being able to stop him.

I need to stop him.

*"You are his wife. Talk some sense into him,"* my father tells me before I leave his house that night.

The woman in the middle, that's who I became. I was the balance, the woman holding together two men with differences.

From that moment on I was used by both. Every time I'd tried to advise Alonso to keep calm and respect my father's wishes, he'd accuse me of not being a loyal wife.

24

I'd been shocked to hear him say those words to me. I'd given my husband my body and soul, how could Alonso have even thought that?

*"I am loyal and devoted to you."*

*"Then help me convince your father that my ideas are right. Help me make him see my point. We could get rid of those that are taking advantage of us, take over their business and double our earnings."*

I tried and all I got was my father talking me into getting Alonso back on track.

I'd been in the middle, and the air had grown thicker and thicker, heavier, every time we'd had a family gathering.

Alonso had ended up out on the streets more and more, while I'd worried at home every night.

*Something will happen.*

*It's going to happen tonight…*

They'd been my thoughts every single day.

I'd been five months pregnant when Alonso had come back home one night, creeping quietly into the bedroom, thinking I was asleep. My eyes had been shut, but I was awake and grateful he'd gotten home safe.

*"La mia bella regina."* My beautiful queen, *he whispers against my naked shoulder.*

*I moan and turn to face him, my short summer nightdress slightly pulled up over my thighs.*

*"Bella, bella, bella." His voice is deeper now as his hand runs over my leg and up around my knee.*

*I smile and curl under his chin, eager for his fingers to reach my thigh.*

25

*"Ah," I moan, reaching up to his mouth. "Everything okay?" I have to ask, before he gets his way.*

*"Tutto perfetto."* Perfect.

*I feel him smile in the semi-darkness of the room.*

*Digging his fingers into my skin, he grabs my thigh and wraps it around his waist, his face diving for my ear first, then my neck and all the way to my shoulder blade.*

*I smile again, holding him closer, my arms around his neck.*

After months, things had seemed smoother, going back to normal. The news of a baby had brought us all together again. I'd been able to see my father letting things drop, seeing how great we were doing, Alonso and I.

We were starting a family of our own, we were focused on becoming parents and I'd felt less impatient, calmer and cautious.

I'd imagined Alonso feeling the same—feeling the responsibility of having a child, setting the example, not risking for our sake. All our sakes.

*"It's kicking," he says placing a hand over the bump while the other one slowly pulls down my panties.*

*I bite my lip, my eyes fluttering, brushing my nose against his. "The baby is getting stronger," I tell him, and even though I can't see his eyes, I know he is looking at me intensely, my body so in tune to his attention. My skin prickles with anticipation.*

*"And you are getting more and more beautiful. I want you so badly," he murmurs, slipping his hand between my legs.*

*The panties are gone, lost somewhere between the sheets.*

My husband is home and wants to make love to me.

*I beam at the thought.*

26

*"How badly?" I tease and lick his lower lips slowly.*

*"Bad girl." He smiles, pulling my hair a little so I can tilt my head back and he can get a better look at me—at my full breasts, exposed by the light, see-through nightgown. "So badly, I'd do things to you, wild things, if only I could get my way with you…" his voice drifts.*

*I bite my lip again, excited.*

Alonso's interest in me had always been high, but when I was expecting, he'd seen me like a goddess, even when I'd seen myself as a bloated, crankier version of myself. He'd seen me as pure and nothing turned my husband on more than an innocent young lady.

*"Promises, promises," I tease, releasing his belt, taking out his shirt. I unbutton it fast and dip my hands in his boxers. Hard, hot and ready, just the way I like him.*

*"Are you sure?" He runs his hand up and down my thigh again, the other one touching my chin.*

*When have I ever said no? Of course I am sure.*

*I look at him, confused for a moment, then smile, taking his hardness and guiding it closer to my core.*

*Making it clear.*

After months of tensions and incomprehension, I'd felt close to my husband again. We'd been smoothing out our issues, and I had him exactly where I'd wanted him.

*"Fuck," he moans against my shoulder, sliding in and out of me.*

*He groans at every thrust, hungry for more.*

We'd been young and foolishly infatuated. When we were in the bedroom, we were at our best.

# CHAPTER 5

I'd woken up to a nightmare.

The police had knocked on our door in the early hours of the morning.


*One look at the officer and I am already shaking, hand over my mouth.*

*Alonso is home; he is still in bed. It can only mean one thing.*

Oh my god.

*I feel my knees go soft as the police officer walks into the house, guiding me to a chair.*

*"What's going on?" Alonso rushes down the stairs, reaching for my hand.*

*I squeeze it tight.*

*"Signora Filomena," the man looks me in the eyes, as I breath in and out slowly.*

No, no, no.

*"Your father…"*

*I let out a deep breath, letting go of my husband's hand, covering my face as I fall apart.*


My father had been found dead in his car, in a countryside road out of Rome. Two men had been in the car with him, all shot in the head. The coroner had told us later on that the time of death had been four a.m.


*"Any idea who could have done this?"*

*I am asked this same question over and over again. But no, no I don't. I… or maybe I do, but I don't want to face the truth.*


Maybe I'd always known, but I refused the idea back then.

I'd wrapped my arms around my womb, around the baby I'd been carrying inside me, and told myself no, it couldn't be. It wasn't true.

My husband could have never killed my father. Could he?

As days went by, after the funeral, after the first moments of confusion, I'd eyed Alonso as he'd spoken to the people coming to pay their respects and thought of the possibilities.

*He could have done this. But how? He was with me, in bed with me.*

*He could have asked someone to do it—could have ordered an execution—but why? Over their disagreements?*

I'd cried in the corner, going back and forth from one thought to another.

The baby had brought us closer, the baby had set things right.

*No, no it couldn't have been Alonso.*

But I'd never really been sure.

*His dark misty eyes drift to me then and he smiles. I know he's always been keeping secrets from me; I know he's lied to me often. I know who my husband is but it is so much easier for me to believe the lies—to believe in the perfect life we are living.*

***

Doubt had become a part of me. It was like a little voice inside my head, a smile, a word, an unspoken word, a sly glance… I'd doubted everything.

A few months later, almost at the end of my pregnancy, I'd been feeling heavier, restless.

My father's sudden death had created a stir.

*"Business is crazy. It's the consequence of Antonio not being with us anymore," Alonso tells me almost every day as he explains to me why he is late.*

I'd started sleeping alone at night.

He'd come back when I was already having breakfast most of the time.

Soldiers were around me all day. I'd felt like I was choking: no space, no more freedom... I'd been a prisoner in my own house.

*"We need to be careful; we still don't know what happened to your father." Alonso asks me to be patient. He is going to find out what happened—he is going to get the rest of the gangsters in the trade to talk.*

*"We will punish the traitors," he reassures me.*

*I nod and smile.*

I believed his words. I'd so wanted to.

But one night, I'd pretended to go to bed like the good wife that I was and waited for the right moment to sneak out of the house. I'd known how: I'd done it before when I was younger.

We'd been living near the city centre back then, and I'd known those streets like the back of my hand. So I'd walked and walked and walked, one hand over my bump, holding back the tears.

It was one of those moments—I knew it was: a moment of realization.

*For better or for worse.*

I'd walked to one of the places I knew my husband controlled his trade from: a night club, dark windows, dark doors, red and blue lights… The man at the door had looked at me surprised.

No, he'd been shocked.


*"You can't go in, ma'am." he touches my shoulder gently, seeing the state I am in.*

*Pregnant, tears running down my cheeks, eyes dark and hurt...*

*"I'm Filomena De la Crux." I glare, my voice angry. "Open the damn door."*

*The man doesn't move an inch: he just stares at me, then searches the street, looking for a soldier maybe to take me away.*

*"Open the damn door!" I roar, hitting him on the chest, reaching for the handle and shaking his hand off my shoulder. "Take your hands off me!" I bark, pushing through and into the building.*

*The sweet scent fills my lungs, the dim lights making me squint.*

*It is loud: music sounds in every room.*

*I walk in fast, through a set of red velvet curtains and into the main room.*

*Naked women dance around tables—tables full of men.*

*I scan the place quickly, frantically, for my husband then my eyes catch sight of something: a set of stairs. That little voice, that doubt inside my head, calls out to me, tells me to walk up the stairs.*

*And I do, fast, feeling the baby kick the air out of my lungs.*

*I reach the top, panting, but I can't stop. I just cannot stop now.*

*Doors to my left and to my right… I open every single one of them.*

*Some rooms are empty; some reek of lust and sin. It is always the same scene: a prostitute and a man, sometimes two men.*

*I open and close fast, darting from one room to another. Until I find what I am looking for: my husband, Alonso, fucking a whore.*

I'd stared at him, my man, my king, thrusting hard inside another woman. She'd been so young, so much younger than me. Her brown, curly hair had covered her eyes, but I'd been able to see her lips part as he'd fucked her on the bed from behind, growling her name.

*"Si, si, Samantha…" He keeps fucking her, doesn't hear me over the music.*

*I watch my husband pound inside a whore. I watch the truth unfold in front of me and let all the lies I have been told wash me over.*

My husband was a cheater, a liar, a man capable of anything. Anything. And I'd let him fool me. I'd closed my eyes and believed his words. I'd let his promises of a rich, powerful life lure me into believing and loving a liar.

*"Figlio di puttana." Son of a bitch. I murmur the words and then cover my mouth to muffle the cry, but Alonso hears me or sees me move.*

*He jumps off the bed, and I have to look away as he pulls up his pants to rush over to me.*

*"Filomena," he starts but I run. I don't let him touch me.*

*I run away from him, from his hands, his dirty, unfaithful hands, his lousy words…*

*I run all the way to the end of the corridor, until he grabs my wrist.*

*"Filomena!" he shouts, pulling me towards him and holding me in his arms, so tightly I can hardly breathe.*

*"Let go of me," I scream in his face, but it serves nothing. He only holds me tighter against him.*

I'm going to be sick.

*"Che cazzo ci fai qui?" What the fuck are you doing here? He roars, his eyes wide in shock.*

*I stare at him, speechless for a moment. I can't believe his words.*

*What the fuck am I doing here?*

"What the fuck are YOU doing here?" *I shout, and he shakes me, his face pressed against mine.*

*I smell liquor, something strong, and his breath nearly makes me puke.*

Don't fucking touch me, don't fucking kiss me.

*His mouth moves so dangerously close.*

*"You are not supposed to be here," he spats out, holding my stare.*

*"No, you are not supposed to be here," I cry out. "How could you? How could you?" I sob, one hand protectively over my womb. "I'm pregnant with your child. How could you do this to me?"*

*How? How?*

*"This has nothing to do with us," he growls, his pupils dilated, like the eyes of a ferocious animal. "Look at me," Alonso says as I turn away, my eyes back on the long corridor—back on that door that I've just opened.*

*The door to the truth.*


We weren't a team; we weren't companions. Lies, lies. Nothing but lies. I was led to believe it had always been about us: he was the king and I was his queen.

Wrong. Alonso had been hiding his disgusting little habit, screwing young prostitutes behind my back, almost every night.


*How long has it been going on? How many times has he come home to me after fucking in a brothel? How many times has he made love to me after fucking a whore?*

*I feel vomit rise in my throat.*

*He's lied to me about us and about God knows what else.*

33

*About my father's death.*

*My doubts, all my suspicions, my nightmares are coming true.*

*"Io ti amo, Filomena," he says searching my eyes. "Ti amo." I love you.*

*I shake my head, trying to get out of his hold, but Alonso won't hear of it. No isn't an option for him. No isn't a word. It is an insult.*

*"You don't love me," I cry out, pushing him back.*

*"Look at me," he growls, his voice so loud and menacing. I turn his way, lips trembling. "This is business? This is what I do. This means nothing, nothing to me."*

*"It means something to me!" I shout in his face. "Get your hands off me!" I push so hard, I finally get away.*

*Without stopping to think twice, I turn and run down the stairs, hearing his footsteps right behind me.*

*"Come back here!"*

*"Where do you think you are going?"*

*"You are my wife!"*

*"You don't get to turn your back on me!"*

*I don't stop. I run fast down the stairs, away from him and my nightmare.*

*How could he? How could he do this to me?*


I'd been a perfect wife. I'd done nothing but satisfy him in every possible way. We'd been thick as thieves, on top of the world; we'd had everything we could possibly ask for: power, money, a whole city at our feet… And a baby coming.

How could he?


*I suck in a breath and let out a cry as my foot touches one of the last steps.*

*My whole body tenses, a sharp pain spreads across my womb.*

34

*I let go of the railing and bend forward to hold my belly with both hands.*

*Another sharp pain, lower this time…*

*I crouch and scream as I fall down the stairs, Alonso's hand brushing against my arm.*

*He nearly catches me—he nearly stops the fall—but he is too late. I hit the floor on my back, then roll on my stomach before everything goes blank.*

*It is too late. For me, for us.*

# CHAPTER 6

*"Signora De la Crux,"* I open my eyes to a bright light.

*My vision is blurry. I blink until I can make out the face of a woman in a white overcoat, asking me questions, a small light pointed straight into my eyes.*

*They've taken me to a hospital, and I am surrounded by nurses and doctors.*

*"The baby." It's all I keep saying.*

*How's the baby? Where's the baby?*

*My hands move to my stomach instantly and feel… nothing.*

*"The baby!" I wail, lifting my head up, shifting on the bed. I want to see—I want to see the bump, the baby. I ache everywhere, but deep down in my heart is where I am bleeding.*

*"Please, please calm down." A nurse pushes me gently back on the pillow, exchanging glances with one of the doctors, who comes forward and rests a hand over my shoulder.*

*"The baby is doing well." Five words that mean the world to me…*

*It's all I want to hear—all I care about. It's all I need to keep breathing.*


I'd gotten to the hospital in a critical state. The baby had suffered from the fall; they'd had to run an emergency c-section to take it out fast.


*"Grazie a Dio, grazie a Dio."* Thank God. *I keep repeating the words, covering my face, crying out for the relief.*

*My baby is okay.*


Nothing else had mattered. In that moment I hadn't cared for Alonso, me or what would happen between us. All I'd wanted was to see that baby with my own eyes, hold it in my arms.

*"The baby is almost one month premature. We need to keep him in an incubator for a few weeks, but he's doing fine. He's strong," the doctor says, smiling down at me reassuringly.*

It's a boy.

*My eyes grow wide as I cry again, smiling, knowing the life inside me has survived the fall overwhelming me.*

*He's strong, so strong.*


I hadn't known how fragile my son would become one day. The weakest one of all. I hadn't known back then that he'd never really survived the fall —that his life would be anything but easy or straightforward.

Alejandro was brought into a world I'd thought I dominated, controlled and ruled with Alonso. A world I'd then realized wasn't real, was built with lies, where loyalty and honour were just empty, meaningless words, used to suppress and manipulate.

I'd carried him in my womb, loving his father unconditionally, loyally, giving him body and soul, waiting for him patiently at home every night, while all that time he'd been sleeping with whores behind my back.

After the doctors had assessed I was in good conditions, I'd been helped by a nurse to a glass wall. I'd seen Alejandro for the first time: the smallest baby in the nursery; the only baby that wasn't crying.


*"He's drinking a lot of milk; he's healthy." The nurse smiles at me.*

He's a strong boy, he's going to make it.

Tears sting my eyes.

He's going to grow up a strong man like…

*I gasp, leaning on the glass window with both hands.*

37

*"Signora…" I feel the nurses' arms around me instantly.*

*"I'm okay." I am quick to smile and straighten up.*

*"Are you sure?" She gives a puzzled look and I nod.*

Smile. Smile. Pretend.


And that's when it had started, when my act had begun. That was the day I'd started showing to the world what I wasn't. What I had to.

I'd been a happy, young mother, and we were a perfect happy couple.


*"She's okay," Alonso says, walking towards us. He looks at me with kind eyes, and I stand still, unable to breathe, speak, move...*

*"I'll take it from here." He smiles and the nurse slowly backs away, telling me she'll be just a couple of doors down if we need her.*

*Alonso.*

*I look at him, so many emotions surging through me.*

*I look at him and see the same scene, over and over again: his whore moaning, him pounding hard inside her.*

*I blink and see the smile on his lips disappear.*

*I've married a stranger, a different man. This can't be the same man I married—the man who said he'd make me his queen, that we'd rule the world together… the man who promised to be faithful in front of God.*

*Had those words meant nothing to him? They'd meant everything to me.*

*What have I done? What was I thinking?*

I glance towards our baby boy.

*He's going to grow up like his father, like Alonso, and the thought makes me shudder.*

*Alonso moves closer then, gets down on his knees and looks up to me. "Perdonami,"* Forgive me.

More tears stream down my cheeks, as I suck in a breath and close my eyes.

*"Forgive me, Filomena. I'm sorry. I never meant to hurt you. I'm sorry for what I did, for everything that's happened," Alonso's pleading eyes stare back at me. "Forgive me. Forgive me."*

You can't trust him. He's hurt you once, he's going to hurt you again.

*Every word out of his mouth for the last few months has been a lie, nothing but lies.*

Ask him about your father. Ask him if he killed him—if he was behind it.


I hadn't been brave enough. I didn't ask then and didn't for a long time after that.

I remember hearing our son cry for the first time, my head had turned to him and Alonso stood. We'd stayed there for I don't know how long, hands and noses pressed against the glass window, mesmerized by Alejandro's wailing, his tiny little hands shaking.

That cry had moved everything inside me: he was my priority; I was a mother.

A mother.


*"He's so beautiful," Alonso says, and I eye him just in time to see one single tear roll down his cheek.*


I'd never seen him cry and never saw it again after that, but that tear, his begging for forgiveness, Alejandro crying in the background for our attention, and my emotional state of mind, had made the decision for me: I forgave him; I let him hold me.

We took the baby home a few weeks after that and I lived everyday convincing myself it had just been a bump in the road, that we could survive this, that the baby would set things straight.

It had just been a bump.

Just a bump in the road.
39

I didn't known we were walking straight into a storm.

# CHAPTER 7

Had my eyes always been closed?

Had I let things happen under my nose, or had I really been so naïve not to notice?

Alonso sleeping around, coming home high and disruptive...

Or maybe what had pleased me before—before Alejandro was born—now scared me, and I'd seen it as a threat?

I'd lived for that moment when he'd come home at night, ready to get in bed with me and make me his: hyper, high on money and power, ready to make me moan all night...

Things had changed. I saw him differently, always wondered if he'd been fucking a whore before me.

*Who? The same one? Why?*

Despite his promises of never hurting me again, despite giving me everything I could possibly desire—maids, nannies, expensive jewellery—I'd never really trusted him again after that night in the brothel.

Alejandro had only been a couple of years old the night Alonso had came home angry, drunk. Something had gone wrong. I'd heard him bark orders to his soldiers. He was loud and rowdy. I'd rushed into Alejandro's room to make sure he was still asleep.

*Soundly.*

I'd closed the door, leaving it just slightly open—enough so I'd be able to hear him call out for me. Then I'd walked down the stairs, into Alonso's office and had seen my husband trashing the place, throwing everything to the ground.


*"What are you doing still up?" he growls, turning my way.*

*"I was waiting for you," I mumble back, looking into his eyes.*

*Dark, red, angry.*

*"Waiting for me…" He snorts, pushing his hair back.*

*I can smell the alcohol on him from afar.*

*"Come to bed." I am about to walk out, back to the bedroom, but Alonso's words stop me dead cold.*

*"Don't you dare turn your back to me. I wasn't done with you,"*

*I turn to look at him again, a puzzle look on my face.*

*"Stop looking at me like that!" he shouts again.*

Like what? Like you are dangerous? Like I don't know you?

What was power doing to him? He was out of control—out of his mind.

*"Then stop coming home like this." I eye him from top to toe.*

*It takes him a second, no more than a second… Alonso jumps over his desk, over the mess he's made in the room and is on to me, pushing me hard against the door.*

*I gasp, letting out a cry, feeling his body pressed against mine.*

*"Don't disrespect me, Filomena," he thunders, his mouth inches from my lips. His hot, bitter breath, makes my stomach clench.*

*How much has he had to drink? How many drugs has he taken?*

*His eyes are wide—dangerously alive.*

*"I've never disrespected you, Alonso." My voice is a whisper and I shake my head a little, my heart in my throat.*

Why am I shaking?

*My pulse quickens. I've never been afraid of him before, never scared he'll hurt me— physically—but when I search his eyes, I can't find what I'm looking for.*

*Where is the man I married? Has he ever been the man I married?*

*"Then stop looking at me like I disgust you."*

42

*"I never said that."* I watch him carefully, my breathing hysterical.

*"You didn't need to: I can read it in those cold, judgemental eyes of yours."* He glares at me. *"You thought it."*

I did. Always. Day and night. It had been like a termite, digging deep inside my mind.

He'd betrayed me. He'd disrespected me as a wife, as a woman, no doubt he'd do it again—that he was already doing it again behind my back, while I was home, busy taking care of Alejandro.

*"I want to go upstairs."* I try to shake him off me, but Alonso only presses harder against my body.

*"And I want you here,"* he says, beaming down at my nighty, at the three buttons over my breasts.

No.

*"Alonso, you're hurting me."* My words fall out of my mouth with each pant, but he doesn't move an inch. Instead, his mouth goes for mine, pressing hard, his tongue forcing itself inside me.

*"Alonso,"* I scream, turning my head, trying to push him back, but he holds me in place— tighter. *"Stop, stop!"*

I scream again and then feel it.

The slap, heavy on my face.

It burns like hell. My head slams against the door as my eyes roll back, right before I am thrown onto the ground.

Alonso is on me in an instant, his hands strong around my wrists.

*"Get off me,"* I scream, before he slaps me again, harder this time, the blow resonating in my brain.

*"Is that how you talk to your husband? Huh?"* Alonso rips the cloth that covers my breasts. *"Tu sei mia moglie!"* You are my wife! *"You will obey to me. You will respect me."* His hands

*snake under my nightgown, pulling my panties down fast. He then reaches for the zipper of his trousers.*

*"Stop, Alonso. Stop!"*

He didn't. He fisted my hair and banged my head hard on the floor, sinking his teeth into my lower lip.

*"You think you are innocent, that you are above me—you and your integrity," he speaks to me through gritted teeth, trying to force himself inside me. "You are just like me. Dirty like me."*

*"Mamma." A tiny little voice shakes the room.*

*"Alejandro!" I cry out, my head turning towards the door. "Alejandro." I cry out his name again, pulling at what is left of my clothes, trying to cover myself, as Alonso quickly pulls himself up.*

He saw us.

*I wipe off the tears fast, a broken empty smile on my lips, while I get up from the floor, struggling to keep my balance.*

Oh my God.

*I cover my mouth and swallow down another cry, then stretch my arm towards my son, a two-year-old, staring down at his mother and father, unable to understand the emotions clouding the room.*

*Alejandro's serious, solemn eyes search mine then turn to look at his father's.*

*"Alejandro." I call out for him again, my arms open to take him in, but he keeps staring at his father. A pure, innocent soul staring at a dark, sick violent one.*

*Alonso steps back, eyes wide, unable to say anything.*

*"Alejandro." This time, he runs to me and grabs onto me tight. I lift him up and let him hide his face under my chin, as I whisper soothing, sweet words to him. "It was just a nightmare," I bite my lip, my voice broken.*

44

Do it for him, do it for your son.

*"Everything is okay, baby. Mommy is going to take you back to bed." I walk slowly but steadily towards the door.*

I'd caught my reflection in one of the glass windows then, and I'd sucked in a breath: swollen, red cheeks, a bruise forming right beside my lip, strands of hair missing... He'd destroyed me, like a broken doll, and I'd seen someone I hadn't recognize.

The ghost of me.

*"I don't want to sleep alone," Alejandro says, his face pressed against my chest.*

*"Mommy is going to sleep with you," I murmur, holding him closer to my heart.*

*Before I leave the room, I turn to look at the man hiding in the shadows: my husband, the demon I've married. I can see the reason coming back, his eyes wide, shocked, like he is coming to terms with what he's done, what he's said.*

*I see the pleading forming on his lips already, before he even says a word.*

He's going to tell me it won't happen again. He's going to beg for forgiveness, cover me in diamonds and gold—try to buy my love back.

*But his words will be meaningless. I don't believe him anymore. I don't believe in us anymore. The trust is gone and so is my love.*

That was the first time he'd hit me... the first of many.

# CHAPTER 8

Our souls are fragile, delicate, sensitive creatures. We are easily corrupted, easily consumed.

I saw my husband's dark soul; I could see it clearly after that. He'd let money and power get to his head; the more he'd gained the more he'd wanted.

With my father not being around anymore, he'd conquered everything, almost everything, and those who hadn't complied—hadn't handed over their power—Alonso had disposed of them.

He'd been so strong, so present and acclaimed on the streets: a self-made man, one of them, a man of the streets. But he'd also been embedded within the high society, friends with politicians, thanks to my father's connections.

Two years after my father's death, Alonso De la Crux had become the King of Rome.

And a king never rests, is never satisfied… his hunger for richness and prestige had made him sleepless, greedy. Alcohol and drugs had turned him into a violent monster.

I was his scapegoat, his release. I'd let him hurt me without talking back, without resisting.


*As long as he hits me and only me, I'll be okay.*

*I get up from bed, wanting to cry after spending the night in bed with Alonso, after letting him toy with me, resigned and remissive like the good wife he wants me to be.*

It's for Alejandro.

*I hold tight to the thought, as I assess the damage: no bruises on my face, nothing anywhere visible, just a couple of slaps across my face, a punch in the stomach, because I'd dared to look at him 'that way'.*

*With disgust, he'd meant.*


I'd been living with a monster and I hadn't been able do anything about it.

A monster with two faces.

He'd slap me and then get down on his knees a moment later to ask for forgiveness, promising he world, telling me I was his everything, that he hadn't mean to.

That it was the lack of sleep. Stress.


*"I never meant to hurt you, Filomena. It will never happen again, amore mio."* My love, *he ays, flowers in his hands.*


A dozen long stem, red velvet roses, like every time he'd done me wrong.

I forgave him so many times. I'd tried to get past the pain, the humiliation, his lies…

Sometimes I'd convinced myself he loved me, in his own way he did. I'd told myself things ould change, that one day he'd realize the pain he'd caused me, his mistakes, and make amends.

I'd waited. I'd swallowed down my pride, my wellbeing, and waited.

That day never came.

Alonso had been a sinister presence in our house. He'd lived at night, slept during the day and ad little, if any, contact with Alejandro at all. During the first years of his life, I'd been our son's orld and his father had just been the man that shouted, the man that rarely smiled, the man with ark circles under his eyes, the man that murmured threats…

So I'd made sure to spend our days out of the house, in the garden or at the park… anywhere ut home, to try to give Alejandro a decent childhood. I'd always smiled, never showed him a ingle tear. Not intentionally anyway.

I'd been alone: no family—my sisters had all married and moved away from Rome—and no iends. I'd been young and alone. And scared. Alonso's favourite felon to punish.

When things had gone wrong and he was high, he'd channelled all his anger on me, like it was ll my fault.

I'd learned how to be quiet, so he'd hurt me less, so he'd be quicker. And I'd felt so embarrassed for not reacting to his violence, so ashamed of myself for not fighting back. But I hadn't been able to: there had been so much at stake. It wasn't just us anymore, it wasn't just me. It was all for Alejandro.

There had been no one I could talk to, just soldiers. The other mothers had kept telling me I was so lucky: we'd been so rich and well off. They'd remained at a distance, always kind and respectful, but the women in the neighbourhood knew who I was and what my husband did for a living. They knew better than to become intimate friends of a lady in the mafia.

So one day, after spending the night with Alonso, feeling dirty and used and tired, I'd thought about going to the police.

I'd taken Alejandro to school and walked down the street, no going back the way I came from. The police station had been three blocks from there. My legs moved fast, determined, the sound of my heels like drums in my ears.

*I'm really doing it; I'm going to do it—to spill it out, all out, and have him sent to prison for his sins, for his cruelty towards me...*

I'd been almost there when my instincts, my gut, told me to look behind, while waiting for the green light at a pedestrian crossing.

Two soldiers had been following me, one of Alonso's car in the distance.

*He's having me followed.*

*I panic, breathing fast, my mind racing.*

*What am I going to do now? They'll tell him I wasn't going home. They'll tell him I was going to the police. He's going to kill me. What will happen to Alejandro?*

I'd crossed the street in haste, thinking about where to go, how to get myself out of the situation when something had caught my attention.

A church.

*Get in there fast.*

I'd picked up the pace and walked through the doors. Candles were lit everywhere. The place had been quiet with no one inside, and I'd embraced the peace, trying to steady my racing heart. I'd walked slowly all the way to the front, to the altar.

The soldiers had remained outside while I prayed, asking God and the Virgin Mary to keep me safe, for my son's sake and to protect him from Alonso.

*"Ti prego, ti prego."* I beg you. *I look up to the cross and hear a creaking sound to my left. The little purple curtain of the confession booth is dangling slightly.*

*Another sound, this time like a foot stepping on wood.*

*There is someone inside, someone in the booth. A priest maybe, someone I can talk to.*

I need someone to talk to.

*I walk up to the booth and step inside, closing the little wooden door behind me. And I wait, heart pounding in my chest, for the person on the other side to open the little sliding door.*

*"Forgive me father, for I have sinned,"* I murmur, my face close to the opening.

A thick mesh had separated the two sides. It had been impossible to make out a face, but someone was there. I could tell someone had been listening, breathing, waiting…

*"Confess your sins to me, open your heart to God,"* a calm male voice sounds on the other side.

*I purse my lips and close my eyes, as I gather my thoughts, all of them, everything I hold inside, hidden from the rest of world. I swallow and voice the deepest, the darkest thought in my mind.*

*"I dream about killing my husband."*

*A thick, heavy silence follows. I hear the man take in a deep breath before speaking again.*
*"Your husband?"*

*"Si," I whisper, crying, leaning over the small wooden table in front of me. "I wish for his own death; I wish he'd never come back home; I wish he'd never touch me again. Never ever again."*

*"Signora."*

*I can tell he is closer to the net, his voice growing impatient, worried.*

*"Has he hurt you?"*

*"Si," I sob.*

Several times. Again and again.

*"Mio Dio…"* Dear God, *he mumbles to himself. "If you want, I can accompany you to the police, call a social worker…"*

*"I can't. I can't go to the police."*

*"It's hard, I know. It's hard to talk about a trauma, a horrible experience like yours. But you came here, you found the courage to talk to someone. The police will put an end to everything, they'll protect you and make sure it never happens again."*

*I shake my head.*

If only it were that easy.

*"You don't understand. You have no idea. My husband would have me killed," I whisper, drying my tears with the back of my hand. "He'd never let me walk away from him; he'd never let me take our son away from him."*

*"There's a child involved." the man mumbles before going quiet.*

*"I couldn't keep living with this burden. I had to tell someone. I have nobody. I didn't know what to do, where to go."*

I'd kept talking and talking. I couldn't believe there was someone there listening; someone I could trust; someone who wasn't involved with the mafia—a man of God who had made an oath of secrecy; a man who didn't know me, what I was.

I'd trusted him with my deepest, darkest secret.


*"I'm trapped," I sob, my hand closing around the golden cross pendant dangling from my neck. "No way out of this alive."*

*"There's always a way out," the priest says, his voice hopeful, reassuring.*


He's a man of faith, while I was a woman of the underworld. There was no such thing as hope where I'd come from. Alonso had made sure to take it out of me for good.

No way out, if not for death.

But I couldn't leave Alejandro in his hands.


*"This was a bad idea, I made a mistake. Forgive me," I say, thinking about the men following me down the street, waiting for me outside. "I must go."*

*"Wait."*

*But I've already grabbed my handbag.*

*"Someone followed me here, I need to go," I tell him, ready to leave the booth. But I stop, biting my lips. One more thing—one more. "My name is Filomena De la Crux. If I die today, please… please I beg you, send someone, social services for my son, Alejandro. Don't leave him in that house alone."*

*"Signora." The man calls for me, but I am already out, my heels thundering over the marble grey floor of the church.*

*"Signora."*

*I hear his voice behind me, but instead of turning I look around the place, dreading to see a soldier, someone, inside.*

Empty.

*I let out a deep breath. Nobody has followed me inside.*

*"Signora." His voice sounds closer this time. His hand touches my shoulder and I turn.*

*Dark, hazel green eyes, chiselled jaw and amber skin...*

*The priest is dressed in his black vest, purple stripes over his shoulders. It is almost Easter, a time of mourning, reflection and redemption.*

*And I've just confessed to him that I wanted to see my husband dead.*

*His young kind eyes look back at me, worried, distress all over his face.*

*"If you need to talk again, I'm here," he tells me, and I nod, managing a smile, holding back the tears. "The house of The Lord is always open."*

*I nod again, not trusting myself to speak.*

No more crying.

*I eye the door, picturing the soldiers waiting for me.*

Time to pretend—to put my mask back on.

# CHAPTER 9

"What took you so long?" Alonso glares at me as soon as I walk into the house that day. The tone of his voice leaves me without a doubt that he's been informed of my whereabouts: one of his soldiers has called him up.

"I stopped by the church, near Alejandro's school," I admit candidly, slowly removing the black leather gloves I am wearing.

I turn my back on him as I take off my scarf, my designer jacket, and stare at my face reflected in the prestigious painting hanging on the wall beside me: a slate of marble, no emotion on my smooth skin. My glassy eyes stare back at me. I have to look down, look away from the embarrassment my life has become.

Nothing glamorous about it: just elegant, expensive things.

No love: just power, control.

I turn to Alonso, staring at him sitting on the chair in front of his espresso.

How did we come to this?

"Why?" He sounds calm, but I know better than to believe the lie in his voice.

Why? So I could tell a complete stranger how you are making my life miserable, how you disappoint me, how you are destroying everything we've built together.

"I asked the priest and the nuns there if I can bring Alejandro's old clothes, his pram and help families that can't buy new ones." I hold his stare and lie through my teeth, with my eyes, my soul.

"Don't you want another child from me?" Alonso asks, rubbing his hand on the table.

My eyes dart to his hand, to his fingers brushing against the wooden surface, and I picture them on my face, running through my hair, the slaps...

"I didn't say that," I pant. I hadn't even notice my breathing has changed, my heart beating fast.

*"What are we going to do?" Alonso murmurs, his eyes losing focus for a moment before they dart back on me. "Why do you fight me, Filomena?"*

*"Fight you?" I shake my head a little. "I've never fought you."*

*"Your disapproving looks, your coldness… you push me away—"*

*I shake my head. "You hurt me."*

*Alonso stands and I take a step back. It's so fast and sudden, an instinct.*

A survival instinct.

*My gesture catches him by surprise—I read it in his eyes, in the way he stares back at me, stunned.*

*I want to keep that distance. I don't want him anywhere near me.*

*"I said I was sorry; I asked you to forgive me," he says, standing still, his eyes searching mine.*

You did, too many times to sound real.

*"I'm trying." I take my time, trying to take in a deep breath.*

*Panic.*

*"I miss my wife," Alonso says. "I miss having you on my side."*

*He takes a step forward and stretches out a hand, his fingers brushing gently against my cheek. My body goes cold, rigid. I eye his fingers as they move in circles over my skin.*

What face is he wearing now? Is it a trick? When will he slap me? When will he tell me he knows exactly what I've been up to? The priest talked to someone or maybe he knows my husband, who I am…

*Panic.*

*"I've never left your side," I tell him, trying not to shake—to not to show him what I'm feeling. How I am scared, terrified, of what is to come.*

*"I bought you red roses—long stem, your favourite—this morning." One hand cups my cheek, and Alonso stretches out his other hand, taking the flowers from the small table to our side.*

*I haven't even noticed the bouquet. I've become so used to receiving them every time he does me wrong.*

It had been his way of showing that he cared, that he was sorry. Alonso had hidden his sins behind those dozen red roses, hid his lies, his unfaithfulness. I knew he was still sleeping with his whores; I knew he spent most nights in his clubs, his brothels. But I was his wife, I was his family, the mother of his son. I was his.

*"Grazie," I whisper, taking them in my hands.*

*"Forgive me, mia bella Filomena. I wasn't myself last night." He runs a hand through my hair and my lips tremble. "I'll give you everything you want. Ask and it's yours, but I need you. Here with me. It won't happen again, I promise you. I need you to forgive me."*

I want you to leave me. I want you to go away. I want you to die.

*For a moment I close my eyes, suppressing my thoughts, and tell him what he wants to hear, what a good wife would say... what will save the day.*

*"I'm here, Alonso." I look up, straight into his eyes, my face stern, unreadable. "I forgive you."*

Forgive your cruelty, forgive your sickness, your addictions.

*"Tu sei una Santa,"* You're a Saint. *He smiles and bends down to kiss me, roughly, dominantly, lacing his fingers around my hair, pulling me towards him slightly.*

*My whole body shakes as my lips part and give in to the kiss.*

Like a 'good' wife should.

*I shiver, hating myself for letting him touch me.*

A good wife never refuses her husband; a good wife is obedient, submissive. That's what we'd been told back then, but what about faithfulness? What about to care, love and protect? Had he ever
55

loved me? Had he ever cared about me? Or had I just been a prize, a means to get him where he'd always wanted to?

To become the King of Rome.


*"I promise you it won't happen again," he murmurs inches from my lips.*

*More lies. Nothing but lies come out of his mouth. I know better than to believe him by now.*

I forgive your disgusting attempt to be a husband, but I will never forget what you've done to me.

I knew it would just be a matter of time until he'd do it again—until he'd hit me, disrespect me again—but there and then I'd pretended I believed him. I'd lied because lies had been my only chance, the only weapon that would help me fight the battle.


*Stay alive, stay in control. Protect Alejandro.*

# CHAPTER 10

Worry had made me sleepless; insomnia had become my most trusted friend.

I hadn't been able to close my eyes that night, too scared to dream, too scared I'd made the biggest mistake of my life by confessing to a complete stranger, a priest, my deepest thoughts.

*What if he goes to the police? I told him my name. I'm so stupid.*

The following day, I'd got Alejandro ready for school and walked fast, heart in my throat, all the way back to the church, holding a bag full of my son's clothes and toys.

*Remember your lie and support it with facts.*

The soldiers had been right behind me—not so discretely this time—no doubt they'd informed Alonso of my whereabouts before I even got home. I'd asked him why they'd followed me.

*"It's for your own safety; I don't want anything to happen to you and Alejandro."*

Bullshit. Another lie.

I knew he had enemies, but the truth was he didn't trust me. A filthy mind like his trusted no one. He hadn't even been able to trust himself most of the times.

*"I'm sorry."*

They were the first words I'd said to the priest as I'd closed the church door behind me, leaving the soldiers outside.

*"Sorry?" the priest asks, giving me a warm smile of relief.*

*I look down, my eyes watery, as he holds my hand between his, enjoying the warmth of his touch. Slowly, I find the strength to look him in the eyes again.*

*"For leaving you in such a horrible manner the other day. For leaving you with a burden, my burden. It was unfair of me. Please forgive me, father." I take my hand back embarrassed.*

I'd told the man I wanted to kill my husband. I'd told him to look after my son in case something happened to me, in case my husband found out I'd revealed his secret: that he was a violent, possessive poor excuse of a man.

*"Roberto. My name is Roberto," he says, letting out a deep breath. "I'm so glad you came back." His stare lowers to the bag I am holding.*

*"I brought you something. It's a donation to the church: my son's clothes and toys." I hand him the bag and he takes it, another warm smile lighting his face.*

*"That's very generous of you. Thank you."*

*I nod, mesmerized by his smile. I haven't seen a real one in so long. "I was afraid you'd gone to the police," I say biting my lip.*

*"I thought about going. I thought about it all night. I couldn't stop thinking about what you said yesterday, how distressed you were when you walked out…"*

*"I'm so sorry." I shake my head, giving him a sad look.*

I shouldn't have come here in the first place.

*"Don't be. I want to help you," he is quick to say, but I shake my head.*

"You have to forget everything I said. Everything. My husband is a very, very dangerous and powerful man, Father Roberto. He knows I've been here. I had to tell him I was here to donate clothes for charity."

"Hence the bag." He nods in understanding.

"Yes." I bite my lip again. "There's nothing that can be done. I just needed someone to talk to, because I was about to explode. I was standing on the edge, ready to jump." I suck in a breath, unable to take in the air I needed.

Panic.

"Please, come take a seat." He reads my mind and gently guides me to the first wooden bench at the far back of the navel. "Mrs De la Crux."

He calls me by my name and I look into his eyes. "Please, don't call me that," I pant out. "Filomena."

Father Roberto nods, giving me an understanding look. "Filomena, you are always welcome in the house of the Lord and I meant what I said the other day: I'm always here for you when you need to talk, when you feel all choked up, ready to give up. I'm here for you, okay?"

I nod, trying to control my breathing.

"Please, tell me what I can do to help. I want to help you."

"No one can help me, Father. My life is nothing but a lie and to stay alive, I need to keep lying. I just need a place to be true to myself, where I don't need to smile when I want to cry, where I can cry and not speak if I don't feel like it. A place where nobody will judge me." My lip trembles. "A place where I can say horrible things, without being condemned."

"I won't condemn or judge you," he reassures me. "Anything you say won't leave this place. And I'm here to listen to your words and respect your silences."

"Grazie," I say, managing to finally catch that breath I've been struggling for.


With a hand over my heart, over the cross pendant, I'd told him everything.
59

About the night I'd found Alonso in the brothel when I was pregnant, how our son came into the world. I talked about my father's death, how I'd always suspected it was Alonso's doing, how vile and evil my husband had turned out to be, and how power and success had changed him.

I'd told Father Roberto everything and when I was done, I'd felt a strange sense of calmness, gratitude and relief. Someone had listened to my story, someone had stood beside me while I admitted everything, my own mistakes, the frivolous ambitious of my youth…

I'd married a powerful Mafioso to become a queen: rich and strong, envied by the high society. I'd embraced the darkness, followed in my father's footsteps, thinking I could fool the world and have everything my heart desired—easy money, jewellery, prestige—believing the devil wouldn't want anything in return, not thinking for one second that he would burn me.

But he did.

And God had been looking down at me, at my guilty dark soul, watching me burn dramatically, burn to ashes as I'd sat in the house of the Lord looking for forgiveness, for strength.

*"Ti assolvo dai tuoi peccati."* I forgive your sins, *Father Roberto murmurs, as mascara bleeds down my cheeks.*

Forgive. If only it were that easy.

# CHAPTER 11

I'd gone back again and again. That little church between The Market and The Ruins had soon become my safe place, my shield from the world, from my husband.

As time went by, Father Roberto and I had become less formal. We'd started talking face to face, sitting on the wooden benches when the church was empty. Some days, when living with Alonso was too much for me to even speak, I'd sit there in silence, staring ahead, trying to stop the screaming in my head.

*You are a lousy wife.*

*You are a lousy mother.*

*A whore, a good at nothing bitch.*

I'd relived the nightmare in my head, begging Christ to wipe it away—to make me forget.

Father Roberto had sat there beside me in silence, compassionately holding my hand.

He isn't much older than me—he'd maybe been in his thirties at the time—but he'd always seemed to have the right words for me to ease my pain.

I'd envied his confidence, wanted his strength, which wasn't about being physical, violent, above the law or dominant. No. I'd learned from him that strength is something deeper: it is emotional and spiritual.

It is faith.

He'd listen to the hell of a life I'd been living and gave me hope. Where I'd seen darkness, he'd seen light. And his arguments had been so convincing, I'd held on to every word.

My visits soon become regular, weekly, then more than once a week. I'd always find an excuse: first it was donations, then I'd started bringing in goods for the nuns. I'd helped them with anything I could, even just for an hour a day.


*"Why do you bother going there? It's not even our church,"* Alonso asks a couple of times, his *eyes narrowed, trying to dig deeper inside my head.*

That's exactly why I go there: because it's not our church; because it has nothing to do with you!

*"I think it's good for our business for me to show up in The Market. Help the community, show them they can rely on Alonso De la Crux. It strengthens their faith in us,"* I tell him.

*Exactly what he wants to hear.*

*Alonso's eyes light up.*

*What a good idea: the wife of a Mafioso helping the poor people on the streets, living in the abandoned, degraded areas of The Market, where he makes most of his money, where he holds the power.*

"Feed the poor, make them see you are on their side and they'll be loyal to you, even sacrifice their own lives for you." *I've heard him tell his soldiers time and time again.*

He'd used me for this too. He'd used me any way he could, but that time I hadn't cared.

*"Donna Filomena."*
*"Donna Filomena."*

Donna Filomena was born on those streets. Whenever I'd walked through The Market, people had bowed their heads, murmuring my name. They'd respected me, the lady of a Mafioso: elegant, sophisticated and solemn, but also kind and giving.

I'd helped Father Roberto and his team of volunteers and attended Sunday mass with Alejandro. Sometimes, Alonso joined us, and those had been some of the hardest moments of my life.

Everything Father Roberto had said or implied, I imagined it was directed at me, to Alonso.

*Don't look at me, don't mind me.*

I'd looked away from him and pretended to pray.

I'd seemed cold and strong on the outside, but inside I'd been screaming, shaking.

*He's here to control me. He's here to uncover the truth and call me out on my lies.*
*He'll figure out Father Roberto knows me, knows us, our story.*

But nothing had ever happened.

Alonso would only come to church for business. It had all been politics, all part of his grand plan to rule the city undisturbed and get the people on the streets to fight for him in the battle against the other gangs.

I'd felt violated—like he'd invaded my territory, my safe harbour—and I'd prayed on that bench to make time tick faster so we'd leave.

But most days, that church had been my breath of fresh air.


*"Hurry inside," Father Roberto shouts, opening the small side door of the church one day.*

*We've been out, taking goods to the people living in the grey, council flats in The Market, when it starts raining, hard.*

*Alejandro is still in school for another hour, so I decide to stay a little longer and help Father Roberto organize the boxes in his office.*

*"You really don't need to, I've got this," he says, trying to take them from my hands with a smile.*

*My stomach flutters like every other time he's smiled.*

*It's more than just kindness, just teeth showing. Father Roberto smiles with his heart, making me feel wanted, appreciated, nothing like the verbal abuse I am accustomed to.*

*"I want to," I smile back, enjoying the warm feeling growing in my chest. I take the box again and put it in a pile, wiping my wet hands on the long grey skirt I'm wearing.*

*We are still soaked, wet through, and I push a strand of damp hair to the side, bending down to take another box. It's heavier than the last; I stumble, a sound of fatigue escaping my lips, and Father Robert looks up. He rushes over, and together we take the box to the corner of the room, smiling at each other.*

*"Easy there," he says, as we put it down slowly, the box almost slipping out of my hand. With a swift move, Father Roberto bends forward and grabs it, easing it onto the pile, straightening up at the same time as me.*

*Our noses brush.*

*I suck in a breath, looking up, meeting his hazel green eyes, and I smile again, ignoring the heat on my skin, the flush of my cheeks.*

*Father Roberto stares back, raindrops rolling down his temples, his wavy damp hair pulled back, the collar around his neck unbuttoned.*

We'd been alone in his office, the place quiet, the only sound in the room being the rain tickling the glass windows… and our hearts, our heavy breathing, his warm breath on my lips.

Our bodies had been so close, and for a moment I'd thought I could hear his heartbeat, loud and steady like mine.

I'd search his eyes again, looking for a reason to take a step back, one, just one reason.

*He's a man of God.*

He was yes, but in that moment all I'd been able to see was a man—the only person I could trust, the one that knew my deepest, darkest secrets and hadn't betrayed me. A man who had stood by my side, ready to listen, support me.

My shoulder to lean upon.

*I look down to his lips and I don't hesitate. One hand on his cheek, I move closer, pressing my lips gently against his. He closes his eyes, welcoming my mouth, his hand reaching for my face.*

*I press my body against his and immediately feel his strong, protective arms wrap around me.*

*"Filomena," he whispers, pulling back slightly, breathing heavily, but I don't stop.*

*I brush my lips against his again, pressing on his mouth urgently. Shivers run down my back, as Father Roberto's hand snakes up my chest and through my wet hair.*

*Our kiss deepens.*

*It reaches deep down into my soul, sparking the life inside me.*

*"Filomena," he moans against my mouth.*

*I open my eyes and stare at him.*

*"I can't," he pants, not letting go of me, leaning his forehead against mine.*

*"I'm sorry." I shut my eyes tight, unable to face him for a moment.*

*What am I doing? What am I thinking? A priest!*

*"I shouldn't have," I mumble, meeting his eyes briefly before looking down.*

*"It wasn't your fault." He shakes his head and smiles again, his eyes seeming a little lost as if he is in search of the right thing to say.*

Confused.

He's confused.

*My lips part then and he lowers his stare to my mouth.*

*This is wrong, so wrong. I can read the torment on his face.*

So wrong.

*But he's tempted. He wants to. I tempt him.*

*"Baciami ancora."* Kiss me again, *I murmur, my lips dangerously close to his.*


Father Roberto had looked up then, his hazel green eyes sinking into mine, and he saw me.

Me.

Not Donna Filomena, not Alonso De la Crux's wife.

Filomena: a strong yet so terribly fragile woman, lonely, hurt and desperate for warmth, something human. Real.

And he'd closed the distance, holding me tight against him.

I'd tasted the heat of his lips, devoured the passion pulsing between us, hungry to feel alive again. My head had spun as life was breathed back into me. He kissed me like I was the most

65

precious being he'd set eyes on, he kissed me like he'd been holding back for so long, consuming, tormented and tense.

I'd never kissed a man like him before, so deep and intense like our kiss. It had felt desirous and liberating, like a rebel yell.


*Silent tears run down my face, and I catch him staring at me, hurting to see me cry.*

*"I can't, Filomena." He breaks the kiss again, gently peeling my hands off his face, avoiding my stare.*

Don't push me away.

*I clear my throat, looking down at our hands for a moment.*

Don't let me go. Don't.

*I look up again, pushing back the tears.*

*I read his eyes. Those eyes don't lie, they never did.*

You feel the same way as I do.

*"Look me in the eyes and tell me you can't," I demand, my voice husky.*

*His grip around my hands tightens as he measures the words, trying to steady his breathing.*

*"Tell me you don't feel what I feel," I press on, not waiting for his answer. "Tell me, you didn't feel what I felt when I kissed you. Tell me you didn't feel something inside you break free."*

*"Filomena," he whispers, and then kisses the inside of my hand—his lips brushing against my wrist, causing me to suck in a breath and let out a soft moan. "You are an amazing woman; an amazing mother. I thank God for the day he put you on my path…" Father Roberto purses his lips, never looking me in the eyes, his head low.*

*"Tell me," I say again, my eyes watery. "Tell me you don't feel for me, the way I feel for you and I'll leave this instant. You'll never see me again."*

I've made another mistake. I'm confused.

*I begin to convince myself that what I'm feeling isn't real: it's in my head, again—another wrong man for me. I try to stand, but his hands pull me down, closer to him, making me gasp.*

*"I fell for you the first day you stepped into that booth." He searches my face, and I see torment in his eyes. "Without even seeing your face, I fell for your voice, your suffering. And then when you left, I couldn't get you out of my head. I fell hard for you, body and soul." Father Roberto speaks quickly, in haste, like the words are too much for him to take.*

*Another tear streams down my face.*

*"You've brought me back to life," I whisper. "You saved me."*

*"I haven't. I wish… I wish I could save you, keep you here," he says, his voice husky as he runs a hand through my hair, staring into me like only he knows how.*

*"Let's stay here. Let's pretend for a moment that we can. That is possible," I whisper, tilting my head back, the look in my eyes a silent a plea.*

*"Oh, Filomena." He brings my hand to his lips and kisses my knuckles. I open my hand and cup his cheek, reaching up to kiss him again, urgent, deep and tempting.*

*I play with his lips, and our tongues touch sending shivers surging through my body.*

*"Love me," I murmur against his mouth, opening my eyes to meet his. "Here, now…" I kiss him again and then search his eyes, my fingers moving to the buttons of his vest.*

*"Filomena…" His voice is hoarse; his chest moves up and down frantically.*

*My fingers are already drawing circles on his bare chest when my lips part and brush dangerously over his skin.*

*He lets out a groan of pleasure, his head tilting back, his fingers lacing around my dark hair as my tongue danced up to his neck.*

*"Ti amo, Roberto," I moan, kissing him all the way up to his chin, then softly on his lips again. "Ti amo, ti amo." I sob the words out like they were ripping my soul apart.*

67

I loved him, and it had hurt, just as much as it had healed. I'd loved again, for real this time, but I loved someone I'd never be able to have, someone who could never love me the way I'd wanted—the way I'd so desperately needed.

I'd been a prisoner, a possession, and he was a man of God.

But I'd loved him, no matter how impossible it all was. I'd loved him in every possible way.


*"Ti amo anche io."* I love you, too, *he says quietly, closing his eyes tight for a moment, cupping my face.* "I love you, even though I shouldn't."

And there it was: the truth.

I'd smiled, never looking away.

No matter how impossible, how absurd, love doesn't care about rules. It's fearless and unapologetic. It moves mountains and shakes us to the core—ready or not.

Holding me tight against him, Roberto had reached for the door and locked it then stared down at me, as I'd slowly unbuttoned my silk shirt.


*I take his hand and guide it over my heart then slowly around my breast. His skin feels so warm against mine.*

*I bite my lip as his other hand runs down my back.*

*"Fai l'amore con me."* Make love to me, *I moan, pulling him closer as I take a seat on his desk. I pull open his vest, placing both hands on his lean torso. Hot and smooth, his chest moves fast. I can feel his heartbeat wild under my touch.*

*His hands move to my skirt, pulling it up slowly, all the way up to my holdups, and his fingers trace circles over the lace rim. A look of desire flashes in his eyes.* "I want you."

*He towers over me, and I tilt back, wrapping my arms around his neck, my legs around his waist.*

*"Even if this means hell, I want you."*
68

*"Si," I groan, eager to feel him inside me.*

*His face moves down to my neck; I feel his lips, his tongue on my skin and moan again, pulling him closer, between my legs.*


He kissed me, all of me, making love to me in a way I can't even possibly begin to explain. Our bodies had sway, mesmerized at every touch, closer at every thrust, deeper down my soul...

I'd held him tight, quietly moaning in his ear, whispering my pleasure, my desire to feel him inside me.

I'd arched my back, welcoming him, asking him to never leave.


*Someone that knows the worst of me, still loves me nevertheless.*


We stayed that way for I don't know how long, until the rain had stopped falling, until our heartbeats had slowed back to normal. Until reality struck and we'd been forced to unlock that door, face the truth and the consequences of what we'd done.

# CHAPTER 12

I waited for guilt to hit me. I waited alone in bed, with my eyes jarred open that night.

Nothing, never came.

Neither did sleep. My emotions had been all over the place. I'd held onto those moments spent with Roberto, in his office.

*In his Church.*

I still cringe a little at the thought.

*God forgive me.*

I'd committed maybe one of the most contorted sins of the flesh. I'd violated the house of the Lord. I've always believed, always respected God and Christianity, but now… look what I did.

Violated a sacred place.

Taken a man of God down with me to hell.

My emotions had been all over the place, yes. I'd been crossed between a new energy, a new found hope and worry, for having betrayed God, condemned Roberto.

And going against my husband. If he were ever to find out… I'd shrugged that thought away quickly, wiping my conscience clean.


*Stop punishing yourself.*

*Stop judging yourself.*

*You and only you know what it's been like these last few years with Alonso. You owe him nothing.*


I hadn't and that was exactly why I hadn't allowed myself to feel guilty.

I wasn't in love with Alonso. As soon as I'd been able to say it, I could admit it to myself.

My marriage had been a charade: I'd had an unfaithful husband, a violent abusive man beside me, and I'd owed him nothing. He'd taken too much from me already—more than I'd ever wanted; more that he'd ever deserved.

During the long sleepless night that followed, I'd told myself I wasn't the one cheating; I wasn't the one breaking an oath. I'd been humiliated both physically and verbally so many times by the man I'd married, that if my father had still been alive he'd have him killed. Or he would have tried to kill him himself.

*If only you were still here, father.*
*Now I know why, why you hesitated—what that look in your eyes meant.*
*Doubt. You'd been doubting your own choices. It hadn't felt right to hand me over to Alonso.*
*But you did it anyway, because of money, power.*
*Business.*

No, I didn't feel guilty. The men in my life had done nothing but let me down. I was on my own, from that moment on. I'd decided my fate, my destiny, and I wasn't going to sit around, be used like a doll, like a prize for a business agreement.

I was taking my life back in my hands.

To sin is human, to forgive is holy and to perseverate is diabolical.

We'd perseverated: we kept seeing each other. I remember walking back in the church a few days later, not knowing what to say, what he'd say, what would become of us.

Our love had been impossible. I'd known it wouldn't be forever. No way we could work in the outside world: a priest and the wife of a drug lord.

He'd never leave his church; I'd never be able to leave my husband.

But between those walls, where no one could see us, we'd created our little world, and it was mostly perfect, but surely real.

*"We need to stop this."*

Roberto had tried to reason with me about our relationship. There were times when his conscience would have the best of him. He'd pace the office or the church when we were alone, ruffling his hair, torment written all over his face, his hazel green eyes filled with sorrow and guilt.

I'd nodded. Every time I'd nodded. He was right—I knew he was. I'd made him betray the Lord.

Do you believe in temptation? In that evil force that drives human beings, pulls them down to their lowest? Do you believe in the good and the evil, as two separate entities?

Roberto was the good and I was the evil. He was spiritual and I was carnal. He was kind and giving, while I'd been demanding and selfish.

I was selfish for destroying his spirituality. He'd never accused me, never said a single thing, a bad thing against me, but I'd felt so anyway.

Still, despite all his good intentions, he'd never stepped back—never let me go.

*"Io ti amo, sopra ogni cosa."* I love you above all things, *he whispers to me in the confession booth on a Sunday morning, just before mass, my husband sitting on a bench in one of the front rows of the church with Alejandro and fifty other people.*

*"Anche io, Roberto."* Me too, *I whisper back, my forehead against the thick net that separates the two sides.*

*He presses his against mine, then looks down at me, sucking in a breath, his eyes misty.*

*"I can't stand you going home to him. Some days, the pain of knowing you there with him is too much to bare. I'd push down that door and take you away."*

*"You can't,"* I whisper back, tilting my head to the side. *"Just as I can't ask you to leave this place."* I smile a bitter smile then placed a finger over his lips. *"Think of Alejandro—think of him. I can't risk leaving him with his father."*

*Roberto nods, resigned.*


There had been no way out, no future for us. The present was all we had and we'd cherished every moment.

I realized I'd fallen in the arms of a man I knew so little about. Only later I'd asked about his upbringing, his life before becoming a priest, and he'd told me he was born and brought up down in Sicily, which had explained so much to me.

His amber skin, green eyes and chiselled jaw, the deep tone of his voice, the accent so melodic like an old, nostalgic love song…


*"I know the mafia, very well. My father was killed by a Mafioso,"* he murmurs one day, as I lay on top of him, completely naked, sprawled on the floor.

*My stomach turns and twists as I make sense inside my head of all the things we've talked about.*

*Take the kids off the streets, give them something to do, a good education, a good life and keep their hands clean, away from the mob, the easy money making. Give them a decent job, an honest living.*

*"I was born where the mafia was born."* I see his jaw twitch nervously. *"I saw my father die in the middle of the streets of Palermo, because he was a judge. He was shot to death for doing his job, sending mobsters to jail."*

*I hold on to him a little tighter.*

*"Vedi, Filomena, vedi."* You see, Filomena. *"I could have taken a gun, found who'd killed him and avenged my father. And I won't lie to you, for a moment I lost my reasoning, my human side*

*and thought of going out on a man hunt. I breathed, in and out, in and out, letting those thoughts rush through me without moving. The vicious part of me, I let it spit venom, yell at me to move and do my father justice. But I never moved. I waited—I waited for rage to become something else. Slowly, it turned into something deeper, something rational and yes, painful. I mourned my father and honoured him the best way I could think of. I gave him a decent burial and found all the energy and strength I needed in my faith in God. I came to Rome, became a priest and vowed to help people on the streets, not wait for them to ask for help, but go out there, in the ghettos, and make myself available to them. Give them an alternative, a way out."*

*"If you openly go against the mob, they'll come for you too…" I whisper, biting my lip, stopping it from trembling.*

*"I can't say what I'd like to say," he tells me. His arms wrap around me a little tighter, as if he feels my body go cold, my voice falter a bit. "People rely on me in this neighbourhood."*


They did. Everyone loved him, but I'd also heard that his growing popularity had been monitored from afar by some of the oldest clans in the city.

Which meant by my husband, too.

I'd shivered and thought of what Alonso could do to Roberto if he'd see him as a threat to his trade. What he'd do to him if he'd found out I'd been sleeping with him.

The world is held together by a thin thread. One wrong move, just one, is all it takes to destroy the balance.

And your life turns into pieces.

# CHAPTER 13

Alejandro had been six when I found out I was pregnant again.

I'd taken the news, hiding my feelings behind that hard, cold mask I'd built to protect myself over the years, where I'd pretended nothing could come through, nothing could get to me, really get to me.

*Another child.*

I'd touched my womb and watched Alejandro play in his room.

*Happy and joyful.*

He'd been growing up beautifully and all thanks to me.

I was a present mother, while Alonso had seemed to have little if no interest in him whatsoever.

Little interest in me also, due to his expanding trade. By then, he'd managed to get his hands on every street corner in Rome, selling his drugs, making money corrupting politicians, building an empire.

Being more and more often out of the house, had given me piece of mind.

We fought less, but nothing had changed.

He'd remained the same filthy, disturbed man, who didn't want me to talk back, who wanted his trophy wife to be his pride and nothing else. Quiet and devoted in bed. Nothing more… or else.

Time hadn't changed Alonso, but it had changed me. I'd no longer been the young, inexperienced woman that he'd married. I'd become a woman that plotted, studied and crafted her own fate.

I'd become Donna Filomena.

I'd had my own friends, my own eyes and ears in The Market. I'd taken all the information I could from the wives of the other mobsters.

That's how I'd found out about Sasha.

Italian, short, thin boned and one of Alonso's favourite whores. Her body had been reminiscent of that of a teenager. She'd probably been no older than twenty, and she was pregnant, just like me.

With a subtle difference.

She'd been pregnant with Alonso's bastard child, while I'd been pregnant with Roberto's child.

*Subtle difference.*

Two children of sin, both brought into this world to suffer.

But I'd grown into a fierce, strong lioness. I was going to protect my child, both my children from any threat. I wasn't going to let a whore and that bastard of my husband hurt my kids.

*No!*

The world is held together by a thin thread. The balance is fragile, but I'd been determined to land on my own two feet, no matter how bad the ground shook.


*I feel the baby kick, right where I place my hand, and my stomach tightens. No smiles, not one sign of emotion or weakness on my perfectly still, marble face.*

*The mask of lies is going to be my shield.*


How did I know it was Roberto's son and not Alonso's? A gut feeling. I'd known the truth without proof. I'd been sleeping with both men, not by choice, but less and less with my husband. He'd started to avoid me.


*"What happened to you? You feel dead. You don't want to make love to your husband anymore?" he growls, getting up from bed.*

I'm far, far away where you can't touch me.

*I eye him coldly as he slips on his trousers.*

As usual he'd dumped all his frustration on me. When things had gone wrong, it was always someone else's fault. Our marriage had been falling to pieces and it was my fault.

I was a bad wife, for not wanting my husband, for not seducing him.

An exemplary husband like Alonso.

I'd hidden my anger behind a look of disgust.

*"Perhaps it's because you've been fucking every woman in town," I snap back, knowing what s to come.*

*He marches back to the bed and slaps me right in the face. The skin right under my eye stings, as if his fingers have slashed my flesh open.*

*I swallow down the fire inside me and hold his stare.*

*Serious, controlled, unemotional.*

*"Or perhaps it's because you continue to hit me. I don't know, Alonso. I just don't know why 'm not so eager to make love to you."*

*"Shut that trap, you cunt." His eyes flare.*

*I smell the alcohol on his breath as I stare at his dilated pupils with loathing.*

*"Never talk back to me. NEVER!" he roars. He shouts thinking he can scare me, like at the eginning.*

*But I'm not afraid of him anymore, not like I once was.*

He'd needed me to be a mother for Alejandro. He'd needed me by his side more than he ever dmitted.

My name had been out there: Donna Filomena had earned the respect and appreciation from hose living in the ghetto. I'd been there to give them hope, to listen to their needs.

I'd made a name for myself. I was still the daughter of Antonio Del Monte and one of the easons Alonso was making business in Rome. Thanks to my father.

I'd known what my position was, what I was worth, and I made sure Alonso would never forget.

*"Then don't disrespect me, Alonso,"* I warn him, showing him just how much his shouts have affected me.

Not one bit.

*I keep my face straight while he shouts the vilest things to me.*

Let it wash over you.

*"My father always said respect and you will be respected."* I speak, despite his yelling.

*"Your father is fucking dead!"* he shouts back.

*"Because he respected the wrong people."* I glare at him, watching his face harden. *"He let the wrong people in his home."*

*"Watch your mouth..."* He puffs out air from his nose like a wild animal ready to destroy.

*"I know you killed him."* I don't stop. It was now or never. *"I know you gave the order, you don't need to admit it or deny it. I know."*

*Alonso glares, standing up, taking a step back away from the bed, not saying a word. Not another word.*

I'd always known, from the very start. I'd known it had been him, just like I knew weeks after our fight in the bedroom that the baby that hid inside me was Roberto's.

Sometimes, your heart feels what your mind refuses to see.

\*\*\*

There are times when the truth is all that matters and we fight body and soul for it.

I had been fighting against the truth—fighting to keep my lies in check. Real.

A woman's heart is a maze, so complicated, intricate and layered.

78

I'd had to hide the truth from the man that I loved. I never told Roberto about the baby, never told him it was his. I convinced myself it was the right thing to do.

*He eyes me, shocked, worried but hopeful. There it is, that look again in his bright merciful eyes. Hope. He hopes it is his, even though it scares him.*

*"I'm sorry." It is all I can say and he understands. The child is Alonso's because I leave no room for doubt.*

*It's better this way. No pressure on him to be a father.*

I had done it for Roberto, to protect him. He wouldn't have survived the torment, his son growing up under Alonso De la Crux's—'The Bloody Colombian's'—house.

Just that year, Alonso had been suspected of killing three major gangsters working in the city. He was powerful, deadly and vicious.

Roberto would have never survived the truth. So I'd hid it well and saved us both the trouble, the worry.

I was enough to protect both of my children.

And that would be my only mission, until my last breath. My children would be my reason for living.

So I set him free.

*"I think we should stop seeing each other."*

It had hurt my soul, each and every word. But I'd had to do it. I'd been selfish and irresponsible. And I loved Roberto too much to see him ache. Or watch him die because of me.

*I walk over to him and cup his cheek, watching him close his eyes then open them again to search mine.*

Lie, lie.

*"Don't hate me." My voice trembles.*

*"I could never," he sighs, breathing in my scent.*

*I shiver and close my eyes, to hold onto my feelings, to remember this moment forever.*


We'd known it wasn't meant to last, but it had still hurt to say goodbye.

I'd kissed him, long and deep, until I hadn't been able to breathe anymore, until I wanted to cry. I'd held onto him a little tighter, let him touch me and enjoyed his big, warm hands on my skin.


*"I've never loved a man the way I loved you." Selflessly, unconditionally—to the point of giving them up to save them.*

*"I will never stop loving you," he says quietly, his lips pressed against my knuckles. I let out a soft cry, letting his words sink into me, deep down inside where no one can find them, where I can hide and cherish them.*

Forever.

*"Fino alla fine."* Until the end, *I whispered back.*

*More than I can ever say, more than you can ever imagine.*

# CHAPTER 14

That wasn't the last time I'd seen him. I kept away as much as I'd been able to, slowed down my visits, blaming it on the baby and the fatigue of having a six-year-old to take care of, too.

We'd continued to go to church on Sundays and play in the football courts nearby after school. When Alonso wasn't around, Roberto and I would give in to temptation and stare at each other from afar, say the occasional greeting.

*"You're glowing," he tells me as I watched Alejandro play with the other kids on the field.*

*The guards are at a distance, enough to give us a moment to talk. We keep it light, conversational, but I can hardly catch my breath, my body shaking from feeling him so close to me.*

So close to us.

*I instinctively caress my bump.*

*I ache for his touch. We've been a part for so long now, months.*

You're glowing.

*I meet his eyes and smile.*

It's because of your son.

*I hold on to the thought, trying to tame my heart. "Thank you, Father Roberto." I clear my throat. He isn't my Roberto anymore. "How have you been?" I ask, searching his face.*

*"I wish I could say well, keep up the appearances, but I don't do well with lies, Donna Filomena. You know that well." He gives me a bitter smile and I look away.*

*A sharp pain cuts through my chest, as I suck in a breath.*

*That smile, his eyes… HIM.*

*He isn't a good liar, but I am.*

*I keep my hands on the bump, keep my hands on the biggest lie I've ever told.*

*And I'll take my responsibilities before God one day. I won't hide my sins, my lies. I'll take his too. I'm the one who's tormented him; I'm the one who's made him sin. He's a good man.*

*I eye Roberto cautiously, careful not to give away anything.*

*"Is he treating you well?" His body stiffens. Father Roberto stares ahead and claps, seeing Alejandro score. "Bravo!" he shouts.*

*My eyes drift to my son, who is smiling and waving our way. "He's never home. He doesn't touch me, doesn't lay a single finger on me. I'm not appealing to him anymore; he has other distractions to play with." My voice trails as I think about Sasha, the prostitute he's gotten pregnant—my dear husband.*

*"Good." He continues to stare ahead. "I have a confession to make."*

*My stomach clenches. I turn his way and he meets my stare. "What do you want to confess?"*

*"A sin," he is quick to say.*

*I swallow down hard and wait, my pulse picking up hearing him lower his voice.*

*"I dream about killing your husband." His stormy, tormented green eyes are back, staring at me desperate, hurting. He is hurting, all because of me.*

*"Roberto." I bring one hand to my mouth.*

*"I dream of him dying, never coming back home, leaving you alone. Never hurting you again." lines start to form on his forehead, as his face contorts with pain.*

What have I done to him?

*I feel the tears pooling in my eyes as I shake my head a little.*


I'd given him my problems, my worries, my sins and had taken him down to the dark pit that was my life. I'd dragged him down to hell with me.


*"Roberto, please," I whisper, but he shakes his head.*

"I had to say it; I had to confess my sin… to someone…" he begins to say, but he can't finish his sentence.

Alejandro runs towards us then, happy, laughing and cheering, his shirt covered in mud, cheeks flushed.

"We won, Mommy." He hugs me tight, his head pressed against the baby bump. "We won!"

My shaky arms wrap around him. My lips are smiling, but my eyes stay on Father Roberto and his serious face.

"Yes we did." I try to smile at my son while Father Roberto ruffles his hair.

He congratulates Alejandro. "You played very well."

"Grazie, Padre." He grins then turns back to me. "Can me and my friend, Valerio, get an ice cream, Mommy?"

"Uhm, sure. Why not." I try to smile again. "Are you coming with us?" I say to Father Roberto.

I don't want to leave him, not yet, not like this. I want to talk; I want to make sure he'll never do what he'd said.

He'd scar his soul forever, march down to hell. And he'd never get away with it.

"No, it's better if I don't." Staring down at Alejandro, he ruffles his hair again and wishes him well. "My respects, Donna Filomena." He gifts me a half smile, staring down at my lips, and then he is gone.


I'd watched him leave—watched him walk back to his church with a heavy heart; his sad eyes.

I will never forget the way he looked at me.

My torment had become his torment.


I suck in a breath and bite my lip, tears stinging my eyes.

Roberto.

83

*I stare at him until he is of sight. He doesn't turn to look back.*

That was the last time I saw him before the baby was born.

Our son arrived two months later during a storm.

***

A mother welcomes her new-born child with tears of joy.

Or so it would have seemed to anyone who had walked into the hospital room where we were staying. I'd held Ramirez in my arms and cried like I'd never cried my whole life. His hazel green eyes stared back at me wide, curious… not a sound from his tiny, little mouth.

Mommy was doing the crying. He'd just looked at me peacefully as he greedily suckled at my breast.

Ramirez De la Crux.

*I scan his little wristband and let the letters sink in.*

De la Crux.

*I swallow down hard.*

De la Crux.

*I breathe in and out, trying to calm down my sobbing.*

He wasn't. He'd never truly be a De la Crux, but he'd grow up like one.

In that moment of confusion and weakness I'd considered telling the truth, giving him away and so many other things.

*What am I doing? How can I let him into this world?*

But then, as the adrenaline from giving birth slowly had washed away, I'd gained control over my feelings again and convinced myself I was on the right path.

*Lie.*

Build a life of lies to protect my sons—both my sons.

Their blood didn't matter. I couldn't risk leaving them without a mother, sentencing them to an unhappy life, or worse: death. I couldn't confess my sins. It wasn't the right time.

I'd straightened my back and done what a mother is supposed to do: sacrifice everything for her children.

*I'll find away to get them out of this mess.*

*One day, one day…*

*I let Alonso hug me, kiss my forehead in the hospital room.*

*"Another son," he says, proudly.*

Another son you'll care nothing about.

I'd kept quiet for Alejandro's sake, but it was true. He'd seemed to have no interest in spending time with his child. It didn't bother me one bit, but I could see it was hurting Alejandro. He hadn't known what his father was—what he was really like. All he understood was that his father didn't have time for him.

Always too busy.

I'd watched my son become quieter and more introverted day after day.

The school had called once, telling me they'd noticed Alejandro's change of attitude. I'd blamed it on the arrival of our second baby. Maybe he was jealous of his brother.

I'd bought some time, saved appearances and tried to talk to him.

*"Your father loves you."*

It had killed me to talk about Alonso like that. It had killed me to lie to my son. Alonso didn't love anyone but himself, but I couldn't tell a seven-year-old that.

*"He's just so busy working for us all day out of the house."*

*"He wants me to go with him" he mumbles, and I swear, every single drop of my blood freezes in a split second, my whole body starting to shake.*

*"Go with him…" I repeat the words to try to make some sense out of them. "Go with him where?"*

*"Around town. He said he wants me to cruise with him one day, in his car, and we can have a man talk," Alejandro tells me.*

*I shake my head, gaping not knowing what to say to him.*

But I'd known what to say to Alonso.

*"You're not taking him with you."*

*"What are you talking about?" he grunts, not even looking up at me.*

*"You're not taking Alejandro with you."*

*"I'm taking him wherever I want, whenever I want," he retorts, giving me no importance.*

*"No!" I shout, my chest heaving frantically.*

*Alonso stands, walks around his desk, straight towards me, one hand in his pocket.*

Don't step back. Don't step back.

*I blink several times, trying to slow down my breathing.*

*He marches over to me, so determined, but I hold my place until he is too close and I step back, right into the wall behind me.*

*"Let's make this clear once and for all, Filomena," he growls, grabbing my chin with one hand, smiling arrogantly down at me. "You don't have the last word in here. I decide what to do with my son."*

*I pant, squinting at my husband, hating him more and more.*

Figlio di puttana. *Son of a bitch.*


I never thought I could hate someone the way I'd hated Alonso: someone that I'd loved, that I thought I'd loved.

Until he'd touched my son, until he'd become interested in him because he was growing—Alejandro had been starting to understand.


*"He'll come with me. I'll teach him everything I know and he'll become powerful and strong like his father." He glares at me, squeezing my chin as I shake my head, making me flinch.*

No, no, never like you.

*"He's too young. You'll get him killed. I can't stand it. I can't stay here at home knowing he's out with you. Someone might hurt him…" I let the tears run down my cheeks, but my face stays hard, like marble.*

*"I care about him, Filomena. Nobody will lay a single finger on Alejandro, I guarantee you this."*

*"You can't do this to me," I say through gritted teeth. "You can't do this to me. You can't take him."*

*Alonso laughs in my face, his head tilted back, then glares down at me again, pity in his eyes. "I can and I will. And there's nothing you can do to stop me, Filomena. Nothing."*

# CHAPTER 15

The next six years were terrible.

I spent them trying to get Alejandro out of the house as much as I could, keeping him as far as possible from his father, but it hadn't always worked.

One day Alonso had taken him for a walk around The Market after school without telling me.

I'd had a nervous breakdown, shouted at the guards to let me go out, but they'd just obeyed the orders that had been given by Alonso: keep me in the house, not let me call anyone.

*I'm going to call the police.*

*He'll get him killed.*

*He'll get him to do horrible things.*

*What are they doing?*

I'd pulled at my hair and shouted the most horrible things to his soldiers, who'd just stared back at me, careless.

I remember rushing over to Alejandro when he'd gotten back home, hugging him tight and glaring at Alonso, my eyes promising him the flames of hell.

*"He's teaching me how to shoot." Alejandro's eyes beam at me as he tells me everything he's done.*

*I listen in horror, as my ten-year-old son tells me all he's learned about guns from his father.*

His father.

I'd glared at Alonso and questioned everything in my life. If I could have gone back in time, I'd have slapped myself, told myself to spit in his face during that first dance instead of falling down to his feet.

I'd fought with Alonso every day from that first time he'd taken our son on the streets, and he'd hit me so bad once, I'd walked around the house looking like a monster for days: cut lip, black eye… no make-up had been able to cover that disgrace but I would have done it again and again if it would have stopped Alonso, if it would have saved my son from his vicious intentions.

But it didn't.

*"What happened to your face?" Ramirez stares at me in horror, coming back from school.*

*"I fell," I lie, biting the inside of my cheek.*

*He caresses my face, his hazel green eyes studying me carefully, smelling the lie.*

Ramirez had had this innate ability to read right through me, his deep thoughts had made me question if he was really a child. He'd been an old soul. Everything about his ways had made me think of Roberto. His real father.

I'd seen Roberto less and less over the years, only stolen glances on Sundays. I'd stopped going into the confession booth; I'd stopped telling him what was happening to me.

It wasn't right of me and I probably should never have, but then I'd look at Ramirez and remind myself that he wouldn't have existed without Roberto. He was all the strength and energy I needed to fight Alonso back.

Alejandro was drifting. I could see how he looked up to his father—how the thrill of roaming the streets, handling a gun and the idea of being so powerful, was starting to take a hold of him.

My attempts to intervene had been in vain.

By the time Alejandro was twelve, he'd become his father's best friend, and I was just his mother: a woman afraid of her own shadow; a woman who'd do or say anything to keep him from living the life he was aching to live.

A dangerous life.

Dark, vicious, tainted with blood.


*"She's trying to come between us."*

*"She doesn't understand."*

*"Don't tell her everything we do," Alonso advises him. "She's a woman. This is our business. This is only for real men, like you and I."*


His disgusting habits, his filthy words had worked.

Alejandro had become distant. We would hardly speak anymore, and every time I'd tried to reach out for him, Alonso would put me in my place.


*"Taci!"* Shut up!


I'd bite my tongue, patiently waiting for when I could speak to my son alone.


*"You worry too much." Alejandro waves it off, not a single word spoken about what is going on with his father. "I'm okay. Everything is okay. You don't have to worry about a thing."*

*"You can say no. You can, Alejandro. If you don't want to go with your father…"*

*"I do. I want to," he is quick to say.*

*I hold my breath, like I've been slapped in the face and the shock has paralyzed me.*

*When did I lose him? When? When had he started thinking so much of his father?*

*When Ramirez was born? Before that? After that? Have I neglected him?*

90

I'd searched for an answer, thinking it could lead me to the solution. I'd blamed myself and failed to get through to him.

*Pride and honour, respect La Famiglia.*

It was all I'd heard him talk about from that moment on. He was in Alonso's hands and it had almost destroyed me completely.

I'd lost him, lost my son to Alonso.

It had almost killed me, but it didn't.

A mother never gives up, not until it's over and there's nothing left to fight for. I still had both my sons to look after and I'd refused to accept defeat, to hand them over to a sick, cold-hearted man, a murder. The Bloody Colombian.

I'd fought. Hard. Until we'd reached the limit and everything blew up in our faces.

# CHAPTER 16

I still can't believe how sly he'd been. Alonso had planned it out so well—crafted to perfection, his plan to destroy me, right when I couldn't do much to stop him. When I couldn't be myself.

We had been celebrating Ramirez's first communion after the ritual in church, and we were in a restaurant on the hilly side of Rome.

Like any drug lord, like any powerful Mafioso, Alonso had wanted a big party for his youngest. Anyone who counted for something in Rome was there and I'd been busy working the room, people stopping me every minute to talk to the hostess: the mother of the young man.

I hadn't cared about anyone in that damn room, if not for my sons and Father Roberto. I'd invited him—my guilty, selfish conscience trying to wash itself clean by asking him to be there for Ramirez.

*His son.*

I'd kept that secret safe from the world, no matter how much a part of me wanted Father Roberto to know.

*The secret dies with me.*

Glancing his way, I could tell from the look on his face that he wasn't pleased to be around gangsters, murders, the scum of humanity all cleaned up for the occasion.

But he just couldn't to say no to me. He never really could. I knew he'd show up: the silent presence beside me, ready to catch me if I were to fall.


*"When's the cake coming out?" Alonso walks behind me suddenly, one hand on my back, whispering in my ear.*

*I jump a little, but mask it well, pretending to move with the music, anything rather than giving him the satisfaction of scaring me.*

*"Another hour. They are all still dancing and there's the salad first," I say, bringing a champagne flute to my lips.*

*Out the corner of my eye, I see Father Roberto eye us with a cold, serious glare before staring ahead, ignoring us completely. But his hand... I can't take my eyes off his hand and how he is holding his drink: like he is about to smash the glass in his grip any minute.*

*"Good. Be right back. Make our guests feel at home, Donna Filomena."*

*Alonso plants a kiss on my shoulder, freezing me in place, then turns my head towards him, holding my chin, and pressing his lips against my mouth.*

*I close my eyes, impatient for him to go away, to leave me alone. He's shown everyone his trophy wife, now he can go.*

Just go!

*I hear him call out to one of his friends before he walks away, laughing.*

Make our guests feel at home.

*Our guests... his friends, not my people...I don't care what he's just said to me. I need a break.*

*Without looking back, I place my glass on the table and exit the room, my long, dark blue dress swaying down the halls and up a set of stairs.*


The restaurant had had two floors. I'd reached the top of the last landing and searched for an open door, a room, a bathroom... somewhere no one would be able to find me and I could wash away his taste on my lips, the mark on my shoulder where his lips had claimed me.

I'd walked into a wide, white marble bathroom and had used all the water and the tissues I'd been able to find to scrub my skin, my lips.

The sound of the door had startled me. I'd looked in the mirror, then turned quickly, seeing a man walk inside the room.

*"Are you hurt?" Father Roberto stands with his back against the door, searching my face* attentively.

Am I hurt? Physically, no. Emotionally, yes. Humiliated, always.

*I nod.*

*"Where?" he asks, taking a step forward but stopping immediately.*

Temptation is hard to resist.

*I watch him hesitate.*

*"Everywhere," I murmur, pushing back the tears. "What are you doing here?"*

*"I'm here for you." Another step forward.*

My heart is in my throat.

*"You asked me to be here. I'm here, for you. Do you need to talk to me?"*

Do I need to talk to him?

*I ponder his words, ask myself that question like I've been doing so for years.*

*I nod.*

*I do.*

*The secret is overwhelming, I feel like I have to tell him. He deserves to know about Ramirez. I want to give him something and take away from Alonso.*

Now or never. Now is the time. Now.

*"Ti amo."* I love you, *I whisper.*

That was the first thing I'd wanted him to know. I'd wanted him to hold on to those words before I'd told him the truth. What I'd done, and that I'd done it out of love. To protect.

*"Ti amo anche io,"* I love you too.

*He walks over and kisses me, his hands holding my face.*

*Voracious and starved for love, our mouths search for one another desperately.*

We'd been apart for too long, repressed our feelings and it had felt like our bodies weren't able to contain the pressure anymore.

Tell him. Tell him now.

*"Roberto." I break the kiss, searching his gleaming, green eyes.*

Tell him.

*It is low, soft, but the sound catches my attention instantly: car doors, then Alonso's voice, then two others—Alejandro. Ramirez—somewhere outside.*

*I search Roberto's eyes then run to the window overlooking the courtyard of the restaurant and behind the white curtain. I stare in horror down at the black car as my husband and my two sons climb in.*

No.

No.

*I turn, eyes filled with tears, and run for the door.*

*"Filomena." Roberto follows me out. I feel his footsteps right behind me all the way down.*

No.

*He can't be doing this to me. He can't. Taking Ramirez with him, now, during his first communion. No. No. No. No.*

*My feet barely touch the ground. I fly down the stairs and run to the main door, pushing through people, dodging waiters.*

*"Alonso!" I shout as the car drives past me, down the driveway, tears running down my face.*

*No. No. This can't be happening. No. He's taken them—he's taken them both.*

*Taken their youth.*

I still remember seeing Ramirez turn to look my way, waving from the car window with a big smile on his lips.

Never saw him smile like that again.

# CHAPTER 17

All it had taken was one look, one look at my sons and I'd known something had happened.

*"Where have you been?" I shout in Alonso's face when they walk back into the restaurant.*

*"Lower you voice," he growls. "It's a party."*

*"I don't give a fuck," I snarled back, challenging his glare. "Where have you been?"*

*I look at my sons, Alejandro quiet as always, his eyes staring back at me a little glassy.*

*Ramirez isn't smiling: he is serious, so serious.*

*"Keep that voice down."*

*"Answer me!" I insist. I demand to know.*

*"Alejandro, Ramirez, go back inside. The cake is coming, go. I need a word with your mother alone."*

*They nod and pass me by. My hands move up to their faces. I touch both their cheeks, but Alejandro stares ahead, resumes walking instantly, while Ramirez hesitates for a moment.*

*His stare meets mine and I see something terrible. Something has broken him.*

How could he? How could I let it happen? Again?

*"Listen to me." He grabs my arm, twisting it enough to make me wince. "Shut that fucking trap. Not another word. We'll discuss this at home."*

*"You are a son of a bitch." I spit in his face, uncaring of who might be walking by, who might be listening in. I've reached my limit, above and beyond.*

*Alonso smirks, wiping his face with a tissue and letting go of my arm. "I'll make sure you'll pay for this, you little cunt."*

YOU will pay. You'll pay for everything.

*He pushes past me and enters the room, cheering and clapping his hands like nothing has even happened.*

I've always been stubborn, demanding and ambitious.

*"When Filomena wants something, Filomena always achieves that something. One way or the other."*

My father used to say that about me. A lot.

Time had changed me, irremediably shaped my character, but not the very essence of my soul.

I wanted to know where my son's had been; what they had done; what Alonso had said to them, and I knew I wasn't going to get a word out of Alejandro, not even now that he'd looked so lost, guarded.

*What did he do to you?*

I hadn't been able to take my eyes off him during our ride home from the restaurant.

Alonso had been in another car—needed elsewhere for his 'business'—so we'd been escorted home by four soldiers.

I couldn't say a word. I knew they were spies, ready to report anything to Alonso. I'd become a prisoner and was considered the enemy where our sons' upbringing was concerned.

So I'd waited, patiently, the bile corroding my stomach, as the anger towards my husband had grown exponentially every time I glanced at Alejandro's blank face.

He had been deep in thought: there with us physically but mentally somewhere else.

*Where? What happened to you?*

*I reach for his hand and he lets me hold it, but he never meets my eyes.*

*And when we arrive home, I let him walk to his room, without saying a word or following him down the corridor.*

*I go to see Ramirez instead.*

*"What happened?" I ask, walking into his room, hurrying to close the door behind me.*

*One of the guards in the hallway moves as though he wants to follow me in, but I give him a dirty, menacing look. "Don't you dare," I roar, slamming the door in his face.*

*This is my house, my son. I don't care about Alonso's orders. I don't care if the soldier will be punished for not doing what he's been told. Nobody cares about me anyway.*

*I want to be alone with my son.*

*"Talk to me, Ramirez," I press on, walking over to him.*

*He sits on his bed, legs crossed, looking down at his hands like he can see something I can't.*

*"Talk to me," I whisper, sitting beside him.*

*His big green eyes glance at me, worried, unsure if he can.*

*"You can tell me anything." I search his face. "I need you to tell me, please."*

*"Dad will get mad at me," he mumbles.*

*"No, no he won't. I won't tell him you said anything. I promise." I am so desperate for the truth my voice almost breaks.*

*Ramirez stares down at his hands again and tells me what I am already dreading. My nightmares become real.*

*"We killed someone."*

I cover my mouth as I let out a cry, gasping for air, trying to fight back the tears.

*Killed someone.*

*The words echo in my head, shake me to the core.*


A ten year old and a sixteen year old…. They'd killed someone.

99

I'd listened in horror as Ramirez had cried the truth out, sitting on his bed, vulnerable, broken and scared.

Alejandro had pulled the trigger for the first time aiming to kill.

*"Shoot him. He's a nobody, just a fucking druggie. Shoot him."*

Alonso had given him the order, staring down at the man sprawled to the ground.

A drug addict, someone from The Market, who'd owed Alonso money. A man without a family, who wouldn't be missed.

The perfect first victim for Alejandro.

*"Please don't kill me."*

The man had begged them to spare him.

*"Just shoot! He's no use to us."*

Alonso had insisted.

Ramirez told me about Alejandro's hesitation, how his arms had been shaking, his grip tight on the gun. He'd stared at the helpless man on the floor, eyes filled with tears, no other choice but to shoot.

*"He killed him; I saw everything." Ramirez tells me, eyes wide. "Dad patted Alejandro's back, told him to wipe those tears away. He is a real man now and real men don't cry. He killed a man. We killed a man. We killed him. We killed..."*

*I take him in my arms, letting him cry out everything he feels inside.*

*He's seen everything.*

Oh my God

*I can't breathe, devastated.*

This can't be real, please tell me it's not true.

*I listen to Ramirez weep, my legs shaking, wanting to rush into Alejandro's room and hug him too. I can only imagine what he's been thinking.*

What if he does something reckless? What if he hurts himself?

*"Don't tell anyone," Ramirez pleads, feeling me shift on the bed, like he can feel I'm about to spring free and run to Alejandro.*

*"I won't. I won't tell anyone," I promise him, holding him a moment longer, before walking out of his room, telling him none of what happened is his fault.*

*It is Alonso's. That son of a bitch. He's lost his mind.*

*How could he do this?*

*I walk fast down the corridor, dodging the soldiers, shouting in their faces to let me through, to get out of my sight. I reach the last two doors when I feel a strong hand grab my dress from behind and pull me back.*

*"Let go of me," I shout, turning around.*

*Alonso.*

He's back. My eyes grow wide as I try to push him away.

"Get off me. Get off me," I tell him through gritted teeth, hitting him with all the strength that I have.

*Nothing. It serves nothing.*

*A hard slap sends my head flying backwards. I hit the wall, but I pull myself up immediately, trying to keep my feet solid on the ground. Only, Alonso is stronger: he keeps pushing me where he wants me to go: into our bedroom.*

*He throws me to the floor and slams the door behind him. "Let's get this straight, once and for all, Filomena," he shouts, walking over to me and fisting my hair in his hand.*

*"Let me go!"*

*"I won't. Not until I'm finished with you." He shakes me a little so I'll look him in the eyes.* *"Bella e stupida,"* Pretty and stupid, *he mumbles under his breath.*

*I glare back at him.*

*I'm not stupid.*

*But sometimes I wish I was, so it wouldn't hurt to be married to a scumbag like him.*

*"I make the decisions around here. I decide where I go, where I take my sons, and from this moment onwards, I'm in charge of their life. Do you understand me? Filomena, look at me." He shakes me again and I glare.*

*"Stronzo."* Son of a bitch.

*Another slap stings my face.*

*"Again? Again?" he roars. "Do not cross me ever again in public like you did earlier, do you understand me? Huh? What do you think this is? Huh? What do you think we do around here? Sell candies? Play with dolls, Filomena?" he pauses, shaking me again, and my head rolls back, heavy and in pain. "You always knew what I was. You knew, your father knew and you know what your sons will become. They are mine. Mine. I'll make leaders, warriors, out of them. Mafiosi like me. Don't come between us or I swear to God, I will kill you."*

My mouth had dropped open as I'd met his eyes. It had been the first time I'd heard the threat, loud and clear.

He was going to kill me.

If I'd tried to save my sons from their fate, my husband was going to get rid of me.

*"Don't make me kill you, Filomena."* He stares into my face, eyes wild, savage, glancing at the bruises forming on my cheeks. *"It would be a shame, to kill something so beautiful."*

Something?

*I close my eyes, my body limp in his arms, and try to group the last bit of energy left in me. To spit in his face. "Va' all'inferno,"* Go to hell.

*And then he hits me again.*

*Everything goes black. I lose consciousness and when I wake up, I am in my room, lying on my bed alone.*

*Alone. I can't do this alone. I can't.*

# CHAPTER 18

Rules are meant to be broken; so are promises.

I'd promised myself I'd never go see Roberto again, but he was all I had. I needed help, I had to stop Alonso.


*Dark bruises on my cheeks, swollen lip…*

*Roberto takes one look at me and his hands turn into fists. "I'm taking you to the hospital; I'm taking you to the police," he says, putting a hand over his mouth, the other reaching out for me.*

*His fingers run through my hair gently. He searches my eyes assessing the damage, staring at the broken pieces of the woman he loves.*

*"You know we can't." I shake my head, looking down at his hand that now cups my cheek. "He owns the city. He'll have us both killed the minute we set foot in a police station."*

*"We should have done this sooner." He's not listening to me, taking a step back, hands balled into fists again. He turns to reach for his coat, his car keys.*

*"Roberto." I take his hand and he stops moving, thinking. Breathing. "I'm not here because I want you to help me," I sigh. "I'm here because I need your help to save my sons."*

*"How?" He shakes his head. "How? When I can't even help you?"*

*"You can," I nodded. "There is a way."*

Another way; not the way you think.


You don't fight crime with justice, that much I'd learned. We couldn't fight a man like Alonso—a Mafioso—with the law. He'd mocked the law, manipulated the rules.

He'd been everywhere.

The only chance we'd had was to use his own weapons against him.

"I need you to do something for me." I take in a deep breath, searching for the right words.

Asking a man of God to sin, again. For you.

My dirty little conscience hesitates a moment.

"What? What, Filomena?" Roberto asks, his voice pleading, his finger on my cheeks again, like he wants to rub the dark marks off my skin, wash away the pain in my soul.

"Help me kill him."

I watch Roberto's face change, his cheeks pale.

"Filomena." He shakes his head, searching my eyes again, incredulous.

"Before he kills me," I go on, "and takes Ramirez and Alejandro under his wing."

"You can't ask me this." Roberto continues to shake his head, his fingers sliding off my cheeks. "I can't."

My face hardens as I push back the tears. "He made Alejandro kill a man," I tell him through gritted teeth.

Roberto gasps, staring at me eyes wide.

"He turned my son into a murderer and he let Ramirez, a kid, watch his brother become a killer. They're just kids, just kids… And he's done this to me." I shake my head, angry tears streaming down my worn out, battered face. "He's killed so many people and now you're looking at me like I'm the monster, like what I'm saying is wrong."

"It is wrong, Filomena. Killing is always wrong," he tries to say, his voice softer now.

"He doesn't deserve to live," I snap, letting the deepest, darkest thoughts out, uncaring of their impact, uncaring of what they'll do to me and Roberto.

What he'll think of me.

I'm not going to hide my feelings; I'm not going to pretend. Not with him—not when I've been forced to pretend for most of my life.

"Alejandro killed a man?" Roberto had shock written all over his face.

*"He made him do it and made sure Ramirez was there to see it," I cry out, feeling all the anger and bitterness boil inside me. "My sons, scarred for life. He wants them to be like him; he'll make them do horrible things... I need to stop him. And I need to stop him now before it's too late."*

Roberto had paced the room in silence, thinking, reasoning with himself, battling with his intentions, with what was right and what was wrong.

Where's that line that separates the good and the evil? Sometimes it's clear; sometimes it's just a blur and you find yourself doubting. How can you fight evil with kindness when that dark force is killing you? Hurting the ones you love?

Humans are not meant to fight clean: we are flesh and bones wrapped around a fragile soul. And we are both, good and evil. All of us. No exceptions.

*"I'm not asking you to kill him," I tell Roberto after he's taken everything in. "I don't want you to mark your hands with his blood, not for me, not for my sons."*

Even if he's your son, too.

*I push away the thought. Now more than ever isn't the time to tell him.*

The consequences of the truth would have been catastrophic. He would have hated me for keeping it from him all that time. He would have hated me for allowing Ramirez to live under Alonso's roof for so long. And he would have done something reckless, something horrible.

It would have changed him forever. I'd disrupted his life, confused him body and mind enough as it was. I'd loved him too much to take him down into the gutter with me.

*I'll take it all on me, on my shoulders like I've done all these years.*

*I'll be the one to go down to hell.*

*"All I need you to do is this."* I purse my lips, ignoring the pulsing ache of the wound around my mouth. I walk closer to him, reading the torment, the angst in his eyes, and tell him everything I have in mind.

# CHAPTER 19

Rain, lightning and thunder had been sounding in the distance. That's the first memory I have about that night.

The phone had started to ring, breaking the silence in the house, waking everyone up but me.

I was already wide awake.

You can't sleep with a guilty conscience; you can only pretend you can't hear it whispering in your ears.

*You are a murderer.*

*You are a sinner.*

*You are a cheater: you betrayed your own husband.*

I'd let it wash over me; I hadn't cared. It hadn't mattered. He'd cheated first, betrayed me first. I'd owed Alonso nothing—nothing, if not payback.

*"Donna Filomena," the maid calls out for me, knocking on my door. I open it and am told there is a police officer on the line, wanting to talk to me.*

Every step I took down the corridor, had been a step closer to the showdown. My heart had been in my throat, but I'd kept my face straight, my eyes blank.

Head high, I'd picked up the phone and taken in a deep breath.

*"Signora Filomena Del Monte?"*

*"Si."*

*"Wife of Alonso De la Crux?"*

*"Si," I say again to the male voice on the other end. "What's going on? Has something happened?" I press on, my voice controlled.*

Steady, steady.

*I wait for the police officer to say something else, tension skyrocketing, and for a moment I panic.*

*What if the plan has backfired? What if Alonso figured it out beforehand?*

Roberto.

*I let out a gasp, fearing for his life, for the lives of everyone involved in my plan.*

*No, no. It can't be. I'd thought it through and it was perfect, impossible to fail.*


My husband had crossed many, many gangsters in the underworld to get what he'd achieved. And the more you become powerful, the more you build a strong, invisible army of enemies.

They'd been out there, on the streets, waiting for the right moment to strike. Only, Alonso had been careful, had mastered the art of never going out alone, never doing the same routes, always unpredictable even when it came to his habits. He'd changed time, date, location at random.

But Alonso hadn't foreseen one small little detail.

I'd known his movements, his whereabouts. I'd studied him carefully over the years, lately even more so, enough to gather important information about him.

It's not just about knowing, it's about giving the right knowledge to the right people at the right time.


*"He's going to the docks, pier number eleven. Tomorrow night. A meeting,"*


Father Roberto had passed the information to a man in the confession booth.

*"That's all I need you to do. Just pass the information to the right person. You know who they are, you know everything that happens in The Market. People respect you,"*

That's what I'd asked Roberto to do for me. Just as I said, right place, right time, right person... Someone that hated my husband, that wanted to see him dead.

I'd wondered how many of us were out there, how many lives he'd destroyed.

*"Signora, we need you to come down to the police station," the policeman tells me.*

*I purse my lips, holding the receiver in my shaky hands, catching sight of Alejandro walking out of his room.*

*"Did something happen?"*

*"Yes, it's your husband. I'm afraid. There was a shooting. Signora, signora?" The man calls for me.*

*"Si, I'm here. Listening, officer. Where's my husband?" I say, holding on to the receiver a little tighter. Even in the darkness, I can feel Alejandro's presence beside me.*

*"You need to come down here, signora. I'm afraid something's happened to your husband. A car is on its way to pick you up."*

All the tears I'd cried had been tears of relief, guilt and bitterness.

For the world, I'd become the inconsolable widow of Alonso De la Crux, dressed in black, proud and devoted wife of a Mafioso.

I'd stared down at the coffin with dark, misty eyes.

I killed a man—killed my husband.

I am an accessory to murder.

After weeks of aching, the plan had finally followed through. They'd ambushed him, shot him dead like he'd shot so many over the years, his life worth nothing more, nothing less. He'd died thinking he was a god, but he too was only made of flesh and bones.

I'd imagined his blood gushing out of the wound. I'd imagined his last thoughts as he'd died on the dirty ground, like a street rat.

Money and power can clean up a man to the point where he thinks he's invincible, above everyone else.

*Look at you Alonso, I think staring down at his pale face.*
*You are nothing. Nothing.*

I'd bent down, pretending to kiss his cheek like a good widow should.

*"Until we meet again," I whisper.*
*And when that day comes I'll tell you how I fooled you, how stupid you were to underestimate me and hurt my sons.*

There's nothing a mother won't do to save her own flesh and blood. Nothing.

I'd fought with every means that I had and I'd do it all again if I could. If I ever had a second chance, I'd do it before that day, before Ramirez's first communion. I waited too long. I'd let my conscience guide me the wrong way.

I never felt sorry for what I did, but at times guilt still visits me, when I am alone, at night at times, but I never let it get to me.

What is done is done; I had my reasons.

But there were consequences to my actions.

It destroyed my relationship with Roberto. He never forgave himself; it changed him forever. No matter how many times I'd argued the necessity of our gesture, Roberto had never truly managed to move forward from there.

Alonso was killed and his killer shot dead by one of my husband's soldiers in the ambush.

We'd played with their lives, all of their lives, liked they'd played with ours time and time again, but Roberto's conscience had been stronger than mine.

*"The end justifies the means," I tell him during one of our secret meetings, but he never seems sure. My words are no relief to him.*

What we had done had worn out our feelings, destroyed what we'd had.

*"I can't live like this," he says to me one day. "I need to leave."*

I remember holding his stare, suppressing my feelings for him, listening to his words and dying a little inside.

*Don't leave.*

*I love you.*

*Please.*

*"I'm going on a mission in Brasil to help out where I can. I need to do something, to stop thinking." He pulls at his hair a little. I see the desperation in his face, the corrosion on his soul.*

*What he's done is killing him; he needs to distance himself from everything.*

*"I don't know if I'll be back," he sighs, staring into my eyes.*

Come back; please come back.

*I silence my thoughts and let myself cry at the loss. I kiss him so intensely, my whole body*
*shakes under his touch. "I'll be here," I whisper, hugging him tight, not putting any more pressure*
*on him.*

I'd put enough on him; I needed to set him free and let him go. I'd told myself to keep it
together, to keep my heart going.

*He'll be back.*

Roberto had left me in Rome—left me to wait for his return.

He'd come back only years later, changed church, and I never saw him alone again. He was a
different man.

I'd stayed in my place and let him be.

My heart had been in pieces once again, but I was a mother, and my heart would keep beating
until my sons no longer needed me. I'd lived for them and tried to change the course of events.

Now you know it never worked.

You can't fix what is irremediably broken. Alonso had made sure to destroy Alejandro's
human side. What I'd done had only stopped my husband from hurting them again, but it hadn't
stopped what he'd started: the transformation of our son into a monster.

I take my responsibilities, the failures on my shoulders.

I sacrificed my life, sacrificed a love, and now you know why I helped Andrea when I did.

A mother knows that a son is the most precious thing life can give you.

A mother knows no right or wrong when her son's life is at stake.

Protect your family at all costs.

I did my best to protect mine.

# EPILOGUE

"Are you okay?" the young officer asks me, his voice bringing me back to the real world, as the memories slowly fade away.

I nod.

I've told him what happened in the factory, what happened to my son and Andrea, while deep down inside I've just relived everything: the mistakes of a lifetime.

"I'm just tired," I tell him, my eyes empty.

"Is there anyone you'd like to call while you wait for the documents, Signora Filomena?"

I nod, looking at the young man in front of me, his eyes strangely kind and understanding.

I'm an old woman who's just lost a son. Who's just been put in front of her darkest failure.

*I have to stop this, all of this.*

"Si," I sigh, pursing my lips. "I'd like to call my son, Ramirez. I need to call my son."

# THE END

## *FIND OUT WHAT HAPPENS NEXT IN CRUX*

Acknowledgements

The amazing support I received over the past few years has been amazing, no... beyond amazing. Superlativo!

Every story, no matter if short or long, is a huge step forward for me as a writer.

I want to thank my family for understanding my craziness, my silences, my need to do this, despite everything we have going on. Thank you Luca, Alessandro and Veronica, you mean the world to me.

I want to say grazie con il cuore, from the bottom of my heart, to Carolann for being a constant presence, a great friend and a wonderful lady. Your daily support in the book world keeps me going. Grazie grazie grazie Pazzerella.

Grazie to Stina, a great friend, always ready to hold my hand. <3

Thank you to all the ladies in my readers group: Gem, Vera, Michelle, Sue, Sharon, Laura, Susan, Melissa, Elizabeth, Lori, Angela... every single one of you in the group. Grazie Bellezze.

Huge thank you to author friends Kiera Jayne, Holly C. Webb, Leaona Luxx, Kate Jessop, Lizzie James, Kristina Beck, H.A. Robinson, Andrea Bills, Yolanda Olson.

Grazie "Beta-fucking-fabulous-readers!" Monja, Stina, Jenz, Gem, Carol.

Thank you to all bloggers and readers, that help me share my work on a daily basis. Thank you for reading and encouraging me.

And last but not least, I want to thank Eleanor Lloyd-Jones, not only for being a wonderful friend and author, but for editing this short novella and Crux. You did a wonderful job and you saved me when I needed help the most. Grazie con il cuore.

Printed in Great Britain
by Amazon

81350415R00068